I Never Loved You

Jess Singh

INDIA · SINGAPORE · MALAYSIA

ISBN 979-8-89066-983-4

Contents

Contents

Contents

Contents

Acknowledgments

So here we are at my second novel. I hope everyone enjoys this better than the first one. I want to thank all my readers for supporting me. It means a lot. Without my readers, the job is not complete. Hope you enjoy this book better than the first one. I promise to deliver my third novel more entertaining.I want to thank my family, who have always supported me. Special thanks to Jay and D. I love you guys. There are lots of amazing humans who have supported me in many ways. Your presence truly makes a difference in many lives. I am one of them. I want to thank Chris and Jane. Jane, thank you so much for all your support.

Thank you, Sirish Rao, for being such an inspirational idol.

Thank you Roshni Patel Vasarm for your support and giving me so many opportunities. I feel blessed.

Thank you Himanshu Malik for your guidance and support.

Thank you Paarull JS Bakshi for your constant support with all the promotional work. Without you, this book would not have been possible.

I would like to thank and acknowledge some of the incredible people who listen to me and support me with anything I need. Thank you, Phil Hanna, Robert Finlayson, and Liban Abdi.

Next is Simone Grewal. You have inspired me in many ways. Thank you for your support.

Kamal Atwal, you are one of my readers who enjoyed reading the book, and your feedback is truly appreciated.

I would like to thank my friends Raj Dulay, Joseph Danica, Roshni Parsad, and Wesley Lawless.

Next are some very amazing people who literally run my life. I love you guys—Stephanie Baotic, Candice Nilsen, and Jennifer Baotic.

The credits for the photos in the book are due to Jose Luis Figueroa Bialy. Thank you, Jose. You are the best.

Finally, I want to say thank you to the Notion Press team, Gerard Mark, and the editors. Without you guys, this mission would have been impossible.

Prologue

GLOOMY DAY

It was a gloomy day in Vancouver. The clouds hovering over the city made the world a little darker. Tara lay in her bed. A comfy bed. She had a very furry white blanket over her. The silk pillow adorning the gorgeous bed with a black leather headboard was white and so were the bedsheets. Tara got up and rested her back against the headboard. She rubbed her eyes and looked at the walls. They were blue. A white table was placed on the side, and in the corner, Tara saw a computer on a table and a leather chair. The single chair was yellow. There was a painting in the middle. Oh! She just realized it was not her bed, she was in a stranger's bedroom, or rather, the bedroom of a man she had just met a night before the disaster. Oh, and she just remembered she kissed Daniel. And he wrote his phone number on her chest! Wow! She shook her head.

Tara got out of the bed. She rubbed her eyes and walked half asleep to the washroom. There was black and white wallpaper on the walls and a small crystal chandelier hanging in the middle from the ceiling. The bathroom was not very big. There was a standing shower and a toilet. She went to the sink and turned the tap on. She again remembered she drank water from the tap in the jail last night. She shook her head in annoyance and rinsed her mouth with the water. If she could, she would use bleach to rinse her mouth.

"Yuck." She gargled and spat out the water a few times. She didn't still feel clean. Tara looked under the sink to see if she could find a brush or toothpaste. But no. She found nothing.

She took some water, washed her face, and then used a towel to wipe it. She put her hands on the sink and glanced into the mirror.

"That was some adventure, Tara... a trip to jail?" Tara laughed. She was laughing, but she didn't know why. There is nothing funny about going to jail! It was like she just woke up from a dream.

"Drunk Tank!" Hahaha, she laughed hard and looked at herself! There was not a single being she could tell this story to. But... she could just take it to the grave with her.

She thought about the last night. She was so scared that she thought she never would come out of that jail. Well! What the hell is a drunk tank? How would she even know? Drunk tanks don't exist in India. Even if they did elsewhere. Girls don't get drunk in India and walk around at night alone. The only thing she was ever told was to stay away from cops; they are bad people.

And here she was, liking the idea of the Police. They had protected her.

"Don't ever tell this to anyone that you didn't know what drunk tank is. Like seriously…" She said to herself in the mirror. Everything about the last night was just funny and horrifying at the same time.

"I want to speak to a lawyer," Tara remembered she was yelling at the police officer in the dark cell.

'All the police officers must have been laughing. Like who cries like that for a drunk tank?'

'Oh well, lesson learned.'

Tara took a towel and wiped her face again and walked out of the bathroom. She didn't know what to make out of this situation. The truth is? It wasn't a dream. This was her reality.

She was in Daniel's house. She went and sat on the bed where she had passed out after a hot meal just this morning. Daniel had picked her up from outside the jail this morning. Her body was still aching from the previous night in jail. What a horrible night. She didn't want to think of it ever again, but could she really forget it? Probably not. Hating her soon-to-be ex-husband, Jordan!

She should be crying or laughing… She was once again back to where she once started after her ex-boyfriend Robin! Robin who disappeared without a word! The thoughts in her mind were running like a flashback and she saw no light at the end of the tunnel.

There were white drapes in the guest bedroom, a mattress on a queen bed, and one light in the middle of the ceiling. It was a high-rise apartment where Daniel had brought her after he picked her up from the roadside outside a police station.

Like she was a homeless girl. Homeless? Well, she had no wallet, no money, and no house to live in. The only person she knew here was her ex-husband.

Tara had a new status now… Single! Ready to mingle?

What to do now? Life had just stopped... she knew no one in the city or country. Tara was uncertain... But she had no fear. Why be afraid of anything when you have nothing to lose? Who knew Tara? No one. She was sitting there looking at this beautiful room. She couldn't go back home and she couldn't stay. How would she live on? She was deep in her thoughts and sleep was nowhere near her. She sat on the bed as she looked out of the window lost in her thoughts... and worries.

Should she call her parents? They probably knew by now what happened. Her ex's family would have told them. Maybe not. They were probably embarrassed to tell the world their son was gay. Tara was angry, frustrated, alone, and homeless.

Just then there was a knock on her door.

"Breakfast in bed, my lady?"

It was Daniel with a trolley rolling down to her bed. There was coffee, a white plate that had scrambled eggs, sausages, bacon, and toast. Tara looked at him. He was dressed in pajamas and no top on. Tara could see the six-packs on his topless body. It felt like the sun shone through her bedroom on a gloomy day. For a moment Tara forgot who she was and her problems...

15

She was with this man whom she had kissed last night, and just after kissing him…? Her life flipped upside down!

Tara took a step back and held on to her feelings. Sexy man, though!

Tara didn't say a word but smiled as she grabbed a coffee…

"Did you sleep well? It's almost evening, but I thought you would like breakfast. Plus, I only know how to make breakfast…" Daniel told her.

Tara smiled again.

"Breakfast is good, and I slept a little bit. Thank you for last night and for letting me stay in your house." She took a sip from her coffee mug and looked at his eyes.

Daniel, who was still standing, hugged Tara and then he sat down on the chair that was next to the bed.

Tara was silent and looked at the breakfast. There was a pause between the two.

Daniel broke the silence.

"What's the problem?

"I don't have a home to go to." Tara grabbed a piece of toast and tried to nibble on it as she expressed her biggest worry. She stuck her lips out and made a sad face.

"You have a home. You live with me," and he paused… "At least for now."

"No, Daniel. You already helped me so much. I don't want to become a burden on you."

Tara who was Indian also remembered that she might be disowned if her family found out she was living alone with a man and they were not married.

"It's all right, babe. You are not a burden. I live alone anyways. Someone stays is no big deal." Daniel rubbed her shoulder.

Tara was so confused. She didn't know what to do. Live with a man alone? Well, her parents married her to a stranger, so what was the big deal if she stayed with this man? Tara had one more worry. Daniel was hot. How would she resist this man?

Tara sipped on her coffee.

"What are you thinking? You can stay here until you find a new place and maybe work?" Daniel was sitting on the chair and his arms were crossed.

Tara smiled, but she had just met him. She had no clue what Daniel did for work. But he seemed kind.

"Ok. Thank you, Daniel. You are very kind." She gave him a smirky smile, but was still unsure if this was the right decision. But what do you do when life is so fucked up already?

IT'S MY LIFE

"Daniel, can I use your phone? I have to call home." Tara didn't want to talk to anyone, but her parents must be wondering about her.

"Of course. Babe, you can use my phone." Daniel took the trolley away. Tara was still on her bed which didn't belong to her.

But now she looked back in time and realized none of the beds she had ever used were hers.

Her parents' house she grew up in was no longer hers. Specifically, not after she would be divorced. She would not be invited back into the family.

She felt as if being a girl was a curse. Tara picked up courage and called her mother.

The phone rang and someone answered…

"Hello," a voice from the other side of the phone answered.

"Mummy…"

"Tara? Where are you calling from? Your father-in-law called and said you and Jordan had a fight and they don't know where you are."

"Mom, I am at a friend's house."

"What friend? Go back to your husband, ok? You get married and you live with your man forever."

"Mom, I can't live with him."

"Your mind is not in the right state, OK? You listen to us, and do as I tell you, Tara."

Tara could not believe what her mother was saying. She ground her teeth as she was so angry at her mother.

"I listened to you guys, to begin with, Mom. Look what happened."

"What happened? All couples have arguments. What is new in that? That doesn't mean you get divorced over a small fight." Her mother was not willing to listen to her.

"Mom, it's not about the fight. You won't understand, Mom."

"No, tell me, Tara. What is it? You have a boyfriend? That we should know about?"

"Mother, I don't have a boyfriend, but Jordan does!"

"What is this nonsense you are talking about, Tara?" the voice from the phone.

Tara was sitting on her bed. She felt more frustrated than ever trying to explain to her mother the situation. She wouldn't know what gay is. A woman who never understood her depression and thought it was some ghost in her body would not understand that a man can love a man and a woman can love a woman. Indians are not comfortable with this conversation.

"You dropped out of college and moved back home and now you are ruining your marriage. Jordan has a boyfriend. So what? You expect him to hang out with girls? He is going to have a boyfriend."

"OMG. Mother, I am telling you Jordan is gay."

"What do you mean gay? Stop talking nonsense. And where are you staying if you are not at your in-law's house?"

"I am with a friend. He is a nice guy I met at the party where Jordan and I fought."

"Tara…" Her mother yelled through the phone. "You are alone in a house with a man?"

"He is a nice man. He is Caucasian and he is helping me, Mom. I didn't know anyone else."

"Tara, leave his house and go back to your in-laws. We are done with this conversation. Go back to your husband."

"I am not going anywhere, Mother."

"Listen, Tara. There must be some misunderstanding. What is this gay? Once you have kids, everything will go fine."

"He loves another man. He kissed another man in front of me."

"Shut up, Tara. You say anything and you want me to believe your bullshit?"

"Mom, everything is bullshit for you. Have you ever tried to understand me once? How do I feel?

You said to get married and I did. I am here alone, suffering, not you. So, from today onwards, I do as I please. I don't care anymore. **It's my life.**"

Tara hung up the phone...

TAKE ON THE WORLD, SASHA

Daniel was in the living room. Tara could hear the sound of the TV. She was angry with her mother. She got up and went to the living room to return Daniel's phone.

He was sitting on the couch and had no top on.

Tara took a deep breath for a moment and then released a sigh.

Holy! He was smoking hot! Daniel had no clue Tara was in the living room. She could notice his biceps, shaved chest, and well-toned abs. Tara couldn't resist looking at him. He had a little bit of beard on his face and his haircut was sleek. He was overall, a ten out of ten man.

Tara walked into the living room and handed him the phone.

"Thank you," she smiled and hesitated. He was a stranger, and she was in the house of this very hot, sexy, irresistible man.

"You are welcome, babe. Come sit here. Let's watch TV."

Tara was still mad at her mother who wanted to control her life. Tara had the urge to be rebellious. She didn't know what to do...

She went and sat next to Daniel on his black leather couch, in front of the 70-inch TV. He was watching football.

"How did it go?" He asked.

"What?"

"With the phone call?"

"Oh. Not very good."

"Why not?"

"My parents don't understand anything. They asked me to go back to my husband."

"Why don't you then, babe? You never told me what happened?"

Tara was trying not to look at Daniel's body while trying to resist him.

Tara tried to make no eye contact. She didn't know how to tell him. Then she took courage in her hands and told him the truth which she was still trying to digest herself. "Oh. I saw him kissing another man."

Tara was looking at the TV. She gave a sidelong look at Daniel, trying not to cry, while grappling with everything that had just happened in one night. She was back to being single, had spent a night in jail, and now she was all alone in a house with a stranger.

"Oh, so your husband is gay and he married you still? How does that work?"

"It's complicated, Daniel. Indian parents don't understand a lot of things."

Daniel pulled Tara closer to him and put his arms around her.

Tara didn't say anything and went closer to him and rested her head on his chest. She could now smell him. He smelled good. Tara put her hand on his chest and her nose against his chest.

Daniel took her face in his hands and tried to kiss her.

Tara hesitated. She was not drunk like last night and technically she was still married. Married to a man who was gay and unable to admit it.

"No. I am sorry. I can't." She pushed him away.

"That's ok, babe. If you don't feel comfortable. Whenever you are ready. You know life is too short not to fall in love and make love." Daniel rubbed her arms and held her a little tight.

For a moment Tara felt like it was home where she felt safe. When a man is alone in the room and he isn't tempted to touch her body…

"Daniel," Tara looked at him.

"Yes, babe?" Danielle looked back at her…

"I don't want to be Tara anymore." Tara sat straight up and looked into Daniel's eyes.

"What do you mean, babe?" Danielle looked at Tara in confusion and rubbed her shoulder.

"What I mean to say is, I want to change my name and have a name that I like. I want to be who I am, not what someone wants me to be. I want to erase this ugly past…"

Danielle took Tara in his arms and held her really tight. She hugged him back…

"You become whatever you like, gorgeous," Daniel kissed Tara on her forehead…

"I don't want to be Tara. I want to be Sasha."

"Well, nice to meet you. Go take on the world, Sasha" Daniel smiled and Tara smiled back at him.

Two months later… Tara who now is Sasha

Chapter – 1

After two months of struggles, Tara who changed her name to Sasha, moved into an apartment in Vancouver with two other girls Nikki and Ira. The rent of the apartment was split between Sasha and Ira and Nikki's parents owned the apartment. How difficult can it be to live with two girls? Not very much. Plus, the café she got her first job in, was just a few blocks away. She could walk to work if needed. A thirty-five-minute walk was not difficult, but then she enjoyed her bus ride to work too.

It was pitch dark in the room, but the sounds from outside woke Sasha up. She opened one eye and looked at the clock. It was just 7:00 pm. She had no will to get out of bed. She worked till 4:00 pm. She got up unwillingly and drew the blackout drapes. From the 17th floor in Vancouver, the city looked lit. She could hear the loud sounds of music coming into her room. She was angry and opened the bedroom door. It was just over two weeks since she moved into this apartment. Sasha was annoyed with the sound, but she kept her cool.

There was a hookah in the middle of the living room. Nikki was smoking out of the hookah and dancing. She had girls over. Sasha didn't know anyone. She just kept walking through the living room, trying to go into the kitchen.

"Hello," Sasha tried not to interfere with the party and wanted to sneak into the kitchen. No one heard her hello. The music was blasting.

Sasha looked at the kitchen counter. There were boxes of pizzas sitting on the counter. She then noticed that a pizza box from last week was still there along with the new boxes. Sasha shook her head in annoyance.

"Who lives like this?" She whispered to herself.

She saw a dry slice of pizza on a plate that had fungus on it. Sasha had seen this plate last week and she didn't touch it. She had no say literally. She had just moved in. It was a shared kitchen and bathroom.

Sasha was confused. For a second, she felt as if she was living with boys. Girls do not live like this, she thought. Girls are usually neat and clean. But this? Was just bizarre.

"Come on babe. Join us. It's Friday night. Let's party." Nikki was dancing in the middle of the living room to rap music. Sasha noticed two girls sitting on the balcony and smoking.

There were leather couches and a 60-inch TV. Sasha was nothing but uncomfortable. She had not seen anything of the Western lifestyle. Certainly not a Canadian lifestyle. But at least she had her other roommate who was from India—Ira. Sasha looked at her room and found it closed. Sasha didn't bother about it.

"Nikki, I have to go to work tomorrow. I can't join you guys, I am sorry." Sasha picked up the pizza boxes and walked out of the main door to put them in a recycle.

'Wow. And I thought I got a great deal in this high-rise apartment,' Sasha talked to herself as she picked up the litter thrown by grown women and walked out of the door.

'A pretty view from my room that I barely stayed in,' Sasha walked down the stairs, still talking to herself. She pushed the button to the ground floor.

"Miss, are you talking to me?" A guy in shorts and a T-shirt who was also in the elevator, asked Sasha.

"Oh no. I am just talking to myself. I am sorry. I didn't notice you," she felt embarrassed. They both stood in the elevator for a few minutes. Sasha had four empty boxes of pizza. She walked out as the elevator door opened. She then walked to the recycle bin and put her recycled pizza boxes in.

"Looks like you had a pizza party," the random guy again asked Sasha.

"Not my party. I feel like I just took over a part-time cleaner job in this apartment I am renting," not making eye contact with the guy she said it in annoyance.

Then she glanced at him.

She noticed a brown guy with a full set of hair and she could notice his six-packs under his cotton shirt. His legs were strongly built and he looked like a tough guy. His hair was sleek and was styled and jelled, nicely parted sideways.

"Oh. Sounds like you are new in this building? That's why I have never seen you before." That handsome dude again interrupted Sasha who was all set to walk away.

"Yes, I am new in the building. Just moved into unit 5854 on the 17th floor," Sasha walked toward the elevator as Vian followed her.

"Oh wow. I am just on floor 23rd. Not too far. I am Vian, BTW," the guy introduced himself as he moved his hand forward to shake with Sasha.

"Is that a penthouse? 23 is the top floor," Sasha questioned him back as she shook his hand. The hand that felt like a rock. Sasha's hair was messed up and she had zero makeup on. 'Jeez, what a bad timing to meet such a handsome man,' she thought.

"Yes. It is a penthouse. Would you like to join me for this Friday night?" Vian asked Sasha as he put his hand on the elevator door to stop it and let Sasha in.

"Are you hitting on me?" Sasha didn't hesitate.

"You are funny. But you are also a new neighbor. So, I am just being courteous," Vian smiled.

Sasha loved the idea of hanging out with this handsome stranger. But she also had work to go to the next day early in the morning. For a second, she hated the fact that she had to work. But then she had rent to pay. 500 dollars was not as bad compared to renting a basement of your own that would cost her 1500$ or more. She had a room in a high-rise apartment and a closet. She could live with a shared bathroom and kitchen. Plus, the view from her bedroom window was worth a million dollars. Who wants to leave that? Sasha snapped out of her thoughts.

"I wish I could join you, but I already have plans. Sorry." Sasha did not like the idea of a guy right now. She was in a recovery mode and needed to figure out her life.

"Well, I hope to see you around." Vian smiled and held the elevator door for Sasha.

It was Sasha's floor and she said bye and got out of the elevator.

A sigh… 'God! So handsome and rich! Ahhh… Sasha, you are not that lucky. Just go back to your hell.'

Sasha opened the door and saw the room full of smoke. The music was loud and the girls were dancing. No one noticed that she had come back.

Chapter – 2

Sasha went into her room and shut the door. There were three rooms in the apartment and one bathroom. Sasha had never seen her other roommate's door open. She had met her once when she was microwaving her food. Sasha wanted to be her friend, but she was never available. Nikki had mentioned that there was a girl named Ira and she was on a student visa. How could a student be this busy? That she could rarely be seen? Not that student life was any easy…

Sasha and Nikki definitely couldn't be friends. Nikki was a bad girl. She smoked. Sasha had smoked and drunk too earlier, but she had never been on drugs… Sasha had no idea what that glass flask they had was. She had never seen anything like that before.

She lay on her bed and opened Google Search. Then she typed, 'flask with smoke'.

Google showed several results, including smoking pipes. She clicked on those and saw the images.

'Shisha Vase' came up, which resembled what she had seen in the living room.

'What is Shisha?' Sasha searched again on Google.

The search engine again showed her the result 'Hookah'.

'Oh, these girls are smoking a hookah?' Sasha was confused and asked herself again.

The sound of the music was still loud. She looked at the clock and it was just 7:30 pm. She opened a book and tried to read, but how could one sleep or read in this noise?

'Meh… what's the harm? Let me go see what these girls are up to.' She opened the door and walked out into the living room.

Nikki was standing outside on the balcony with two other friends of hers. The balcony was a little small. It could just fit a little furniture and a couple of people.

"Hey Sasha, you woke up? Come hang out with us."

How could Sasha say no? Someone was so polite to ask. After all, she was new to this world and she had no friends. Sasha took her chances.

Sasha opened the sliding door and walked out onto the balcony. She took a chair.

"Hey, girl! You finally awake?" Nikki passed her wine glass to Sasha.

Sasha took the wine glass and had a sip.

"Yes. I thought I could hang out for a few hours, I guess." Sasha said.

"Well, that is great, honey. Meet my friends, Sierra and Amber. Guys, she is my new roommate Sasha." Nikki took another puff from something that looked like a cigarette.

"Hello," Sasha was shy and hesitant. She could smell the smoke and it smelled like a skunk. A Canadian animal skunk. She had smelled skunk many times and did not like the smell.

"You want to take a Toke (puff) babe?" Nikki offered the roll-up that looked like a cigarette.

"No, thank you. I am okay," Sasha was hesitant as she did not want to take any drugs.

"Babe, it's just weed. Just have some, and it will relax your mind," Nikki insisted.

Sasha was hesitant, but she had smoked before when she wanted to be a bad girl. So why not now?

She accepted the roll and took a puff and then another puff.

"That's my girl!" Nikki took the roll-up back, had a puff and passed it on to her friends Sierra and Amber who were Caucasian and had blond hair.

Sasha's eyes dilated and she could feel the high as she looked at the city again. It was now more lit up than ever. She sat quietly and listened to her roommate's conversation as she sipped the wine…

The girls were talking about some party. Sasha could only pay attention to some bits of the conversation.

'So, this is the new world?' Sasha was high… She had never been high before.

Sasha joined the smoking session as the roll-up was passed among them. She was drunk and high on weed. And lost in her thoughts… She again thought of Vian. She now wished she had accepted his offer. Oh well!

No one to question and no one to answer to. It was just Sasha who had to decide what was good or bad. Right now, she was bad… she picked up the wine glass and returned to the living room. All three girls followed her…

Chapter – 3

The alarm rang at 6 a.m. The sun was bright and peeking through her window... mmm... another beautiful day. Sasha opened one eye. She didn't want to get up, but she had work..

'Ahhhhh headache,' she spoke to herself and realized she had been drunk last night. Actually, she didn't even know if she had slept or if she was just intoxicated and lying in bed. And she had smoked weed. Sasha felt guilty over having smoked weed.

'Oh. I just did drugs. Bad girl,' Sasha whispered to herself.

"Lord Shiva smoked weed. So, how is that bad?" She tried to justify her recent sin, but she also had a new friend, Nikki.

She exited bed, grabbed her toothbrush, and quietly opened her bedroom door. She had already forgotten the name of the girl still lying on the sofa and Nikki's door was shut. She brushed her teeth and took a shower. She tried to make no sounds… everyone was still sleeping. She wished she could sleep too, but then she had to make money to pay rent and feed herself.

She grabbed her lunch, pulled her hair up, and exited the door.

Sasha got in the elevator with her backpack which seemed heavier than life!

She got out on the ground floor and noticed a girl hugging a middle-aged man. That was her other roommate, Ira.

"Hello," Sasha stopped and greeted her.

Ira pushed the man away from her and looked at Sasha.

"Hello," Ira said.

There was no one in the lobby. Just Ira, Sasha, and that middle-aged man.

Sasha looked at the man.

"He is my uncle, Jatin. He lives in Richmond with his family. He came to drop me off after my graveyard shift," Ira was hesitant.

"Hello," Sasha said, finding the whole information shady.

"I must go to work. I will talk to you later," she said. Sasha didn't know her. She was her roommate who was never home and if she was at home, her bedroom door was usually shut.

Ira was skinny and about 5'3". Sasha glanced at her. She was wearing Guess shoes and an expensive watch, and it seemed like she had an LV bag. Sasha was surprised how a girl on a student visa could afford all these luxurious things. Maybe she belonged to some rich family in India. Who knows?

Sasha was a little envious, but could not indulge in those feelings for long. She had a job she needed to take care of that paid her minimum wage. Oh well… What can you do when you live in a shoe?

"Ok," Ira replied.

"Oh. Nikki and her friends are still up there sleeping," Sasha warned her.

"It's ok. I am used to it. I have been living with her for over six months now," Ira smiled and again cut it short.

"Ok, I better leave; otherwise, I will be late for work," Sasha pulled up her bags a little more.

"I can drop you off at your work if you like?" Jatin asked.

"I thought you had a meeting after dropping me off?" Ira interrupted and raised her eyebrows.

"It's ok. I will manage. Thank you," Sasha said bye and walked out of the building.

The café was not far from where she lived. She could take a walk and be there on time.

Chapter – 4

"You are late, Sasha," Sukh, an older man in his late forties, questioned Sasha.

"I am sorry, Sukh. Won't happen again." Sasha put her bag down in the café where she worked as a server. This elegant café, which was open from 9:00 a.m. to 9:00 p.m. was located in the heart of Vancouver.

Sasha went ahead and changed, and came out wearing an apron.

"It's ok, baby girl. Sukh has been getting bitter over the years. But he has a good heart," said Mike, a Caucasian man who ran the show for Sukh. Sasha saw him every day. He greeted customers like it was his house.

Sasha just wondered each day how come someone so handsome and nice was working in a café serving people every day. Mike was 6'2" tall and wore a white shirt and blue pants daily. He walked with his shoulders low and when he smiled, his lips had a line around them, but his muscular jaw made him look handsome.

'What an irony! I am late one day and he is already here?' Sasha put a knot on her apron and started putting the dirty glasses in the dishwasher as she mumbled.

The café was usually busy during the mornings and the lunch hours. Two other people were working in the café. One was a guy named Patrick who was also Caucasian, a boy in his early twenties. Sasha found Patrick a little strange. He wore tattoos over his sleeve, and his nails were painted black. All the time. His head was shaved on both sides, and his hair was up in a mohawk.

"Hi," Sasha greeted Patrick who was making coffee for a customer.

Patrick turned his neck around while his hand was still under the coffee machine.

"Yo, what's up? You made it!"

"Yes, I did and I had to see Sukh."

"Ahh, don't worry about him, babe. He is like that. You know how many times I got into shit. Like in the past month? Five times."

Patrick handed in the coffee to the waiting customer.

"Thank you," said the customer.

"See you next time. Next customer," Patrick raised his hand.

Sasha was done with putting dishes in the washer. The café was getting busier.

"Babe, can you please take over the till? I am just going out for a smoke," Patrick politely asked Sasha as he took the apron off.

"Yes, sure," Sasha smiled.

"Watch out for the boys, babe," Patrick laughed as he walked out the door.

"Go away, Patrick," Sasha told him off as she smiled and shied away.

In the beginning, Sasha would take offense, but it took her a couple of days to understand that he was joking.

The other staff member was another Indian girl who never bothered speaking to Sasha.

She looked like she was in her early twenties. Sasha could tell she was born and raised here in Canada. She spoke fluent English and had no accent. She dressed well and was petite in size. She was quiet, keeping to herself. Who knows why she was so quiet? But the boys liked her. Both Patrick and Mike.

The struggle of being in the new city was not just finding work and trying to live a normal life. It was more than that. You had to make new friends all over again, then you had to try to find someone you could trust… There was no family here. You were missing out on so many things… all together while you try to make a living.

Sasha remembered her past and she also tried to forget it at the same time.

There was a customer at the till.

"Hello. How can I help you," Sasha tried not to make eye contact with this guy.

'God! He is so hot!' A whole trail of thoughts was going through her mind. A brown man, he had dimples on his cheeks and black lush hair. His chest looked pretty ripped in the white shirt he wore that was well paired with blue jeans. His biceps were very visible. Even though Sasha tried not to look at him, she made eye contact and nodded for him to speak, as she was ready to take the order.

"One caramel macchiato with a toasted bagel with cream and butter."

Sasha was so lost in her thoughts that she skipped the whole order.

"I am sorry, sir. Can you please repeat your order?" Sasha still tried not to make any eye contact.

"One caramel macchiato and toasted bagel with cream cheese," the stranger spoke.

"That's all?" Sasha looked at him as he spoke.

"Anything else I can help you with, Sir?" Sasha tapped out the order.

"No. That's all. Thank you, Sasha."

'What? He knows my name?' Sasha was shocked until she realized she was wearing her name tag. And felt stupid for a second.

"Your total comes to six dollars and seventeen cents. How would you like to pay?"

"With debit card."

"Please insert at the bottom," Tara showed him the swipe machine.

The man smiled… "You know how funny that sounds?"

"Funny what?" Sasha looked at him while giving him his receipt.

"Never mind. Thank you," he winked at Sasha and left.

"Did you see him? Oh, my goodness!" Sasha took a deep breath.

"Yeah, he was a handsome fella. Even I would do him. You should have asked his number, Sasha."

"You are silly, Patrick. This is not how it works."

"This is exactly how it works. Have you not dated before?"

"Well, not exactly, but I have been dated. If hanging out with a man is counted as dating?" Sasha looked at him.

And now the question lingered over her mind. 'What if she did want to date another man? Would he accept her? No matter where you go or how much you try to hide, the darkness in life will find you...'

Sasha was silent and lost in her thoughts.

Just then a sound interrupted her thoughts.

"Hey. This is my business card. Call me!" Just then, that man came back and gave Sasha his card. Sasha didn't know what to say or respond... She took the card and glanced at it.

"Oh. Rahul... mm... a real estate agent! Wow." Patrick took the card away from Sasha's hands and teased her.

"Give it back to me, Patrick," Sasha snatched the card from him and put it in her pocket. And she smiled. Her dimples were more prominent when she smiled.

"Sasha, be careful trusting people this quick," Patrick gave her a grim look and a smirky smile.

"You have to trust someone someday? No?" She smiled and her dimples appeared again.

Patrick pulled his boxers up and returned to the till to take the orders. The line-up was getting bigger.

"Hello. Can I please get a bagel and a brown sugar oats Americano?"–the customer who stood there seemed annoyed.

"Sure, and your total comes up to 8.67$." Patrick looked at the screen.

Chapter – 5

It was late in the evening. Sasha walked out of the café. The streets of Vancouver were quite busy. She saw people walking around. Her shift was over. Now what? She was tired from working all day, but then there was nothing she was looking forward to in going back to her room. Maybe some TV watching with a bowl of Mr. Noodles. Her everyday meal. That was all that she could afford. But working at the café had some perks. The owner allowed them to get food sometimes, which was the only gourmet meal she could afford, and she thoroughly enjoyed it.

She missed home. How her mother cooked and the whole house smelled like food and she got to just stay in her bed and enjoy the lavish meals while she watched her favorite Indian TV shows.

But there was no home here. Everything and everyone were strangers. The people, the streets, the food, the TV shows, the air she was breathing in. Alone in a city full of people.

She took out the business card that she was handed. She glanced at it. Should she give him a call? It was very late in the evening. What would he think? Sasha's thoughts were all over the place. She would have to eventually find someone she could trust. You take your chances. Finding love in life was just like gambling. You either lose it all or you gain it all. There is no gray. Some days it hurts and some days it takes you to cloud nine. She wanted to be in love with someone. Could this be that someone? When you are single, every man seems like a potential husband. You know what they say? You have to kiss many frogs before you meet your prince.

She could walk back home and kill some time.

But then she was tempted to kill this loneliness she had been living with and no one to call a friend. Sasha took her phone out and dialed the number, in desperate need of some human interaction.

"Hello," a voice from the other side.

"Hi," Sasha responded.

"Who is this?" A man's voice from the phone.

"This is Sasha from the café. Sorry, it's too late, but I just got off work."

"Oh no, no. Not at all. I was lying in bed thinking of you. I am glad you called. So, what's going on?" The man asked.

"Oh, I just wanted to say hello and thank you for the business card."

"Not a problem. You are off to home or want to meet up? What is in the mind?"

"Well. I am off to home. Just taking a walk back."

"You want me to join you?"

Sasha realized she was dirty, stinky, and tired after work. She should not meet someone so hot in this state. Looking and feeling like this.

"Well. It's late. Isn't? I thought I would just give you a call."

"I am glad you did. We can meet up tomorrow? I don't have a lot on my schedule."

"Sure. That sounds good."

"And we can be friends with benefits."

"Yes, for sure. I would love to have friends with benefits."

"Well then. In that case, we have a date tomorrow. I will text you the time and location."

"Sounds great. Thank you."

Sasha hung up the phone. The night looked more beautiful. Now she had a friend with benefits!

Sasha loved this concept. She could help the guy with his work and at the same time, they could hang out. Sasha had many thoughts in her mind.

'Finally, I have a friend. Now we can hang out together and I can learn things from him. Thank you, God. I am really happy.' Sasha walked a little faster to her apartment. There was happiness in her heart. In this big world, she was alone.

Not anymore! She would be helping this man with his real estate work while they hung out like friends. Constantly looking for opportunities and trying to make new friends. Sasha did not give a second thought about what friends with benefits could mean. For her it was simple English… you help someone and they help you!

Whoa!

Chapter – 6

Sasha entered her building. The night was still bright.

She took the elevator.

"Oh, hey, can you hold the door for me?" Sasha put her foot in the door and the elevator door opened again.

It was him again… the penthouse guy. Very handsome. He was dressed so well in a gray suit, black tie, and hair nicely cute and parted onto one side.

Sasha looked up again and heaved a big sigh.

"Oh, hello, Sasha. How have you been?" Vian, the penthouse guy asked her.

Not wanting to tell him, Sasha had no choice. She was dirty after work and looked exhausted.

"Oh hello," she had already forgotten his name. Well, she never thought she would meet him again.

"Which floor?" Sasha asked.

"Oh, the penthouse," Vian moved his bag from one shoulder to the other.

"Oh of course. I forgot."

"You remember my name, right?" Sasha went red and blushed in embarrassment. She had forgotten this guy's name. What was the point in remembering his name? It's not like she had a chance with this handsome-looking man who was very successful. He lived in a penthouse, and she lived with two other girls and worked at a café!

"I am sorry, I can't recall your name. I am really tired from work."

"It's Vian. Here, take my number and call me sometimes. I can show you around my penthouse." Vian took a card out and handed it to Sasha. Just then "ding". It was her floor.

"See you again, Sasha," Vian waved at her and waited for the elevator door to close.

Sasha held the card and walked up to her apartment.

She quietly put the key in and opened the door. The room was bright and Nikki was awake. The TV was loud and weird sounds were coming from the other room! Ira's room. She was moaning.

"Hey." Nikki was sipping beer and watching TV. The living room was messy. There was food everywhere. Sasha was disgusted but didn't say anything. She couldn't. This was the price you had to pay for cheap rent.

Maybe it was a habit? Maybe Nikki drank every evening?

"Hello. You want me to get you something to eat, Nikki?"

"No, babe. I am fine. Don't want to wear down the effect of booze," Nikki took another sip of her beer.

"It's not good for you to have just a drink." Sasha took her food out and warmed it up. Then she went and sat next to Nikki with her food.

"It's ok, babe. My body is used to it," Nikki laughed again.

"You don't get tired?" Sasha questioned and tried to figure out how she was still awake.

"You do lines, babe? You can stay awake as long as you want. I just spent Gino!" Nikki took a sip.

Sasha was more confused than ever. Lines? What did lines mean? And what did Gino mean?

Life was easy. She knew the English language well, but the words Nikki was using? Sasha had never heard those before. She was surprised how Nikki could drink and no one told her anything, and here she was, who had hidden whiskey from her dad to drink it secretly. She used to top the bottle with water so her dad could never find out she stole alcohol from his bottles.

Sasha smiled… thinking of her being so clever, stealing alcohol from her dad, and now she felt stupid in this new world where everything was new...

Sasha did not want to ask Nikki what she was referring to when she said those lines. She might laugh at her. Who could she ask all this?

Oh, she had a friend with benefits… she would ask him what all this meant. Sasha smiled.

"Nikki… Can you please lower the sound of the TV? It's so loud and deafening. I want to relax before I go to sleep," Sasha nicely asked Nikki.

"Oh, sure, babe. But don't blame me if you hear loud sounds other than from the TV," there was sarcasm in her tone.

"Scream louder so your friend can hear you scream, baby," the sound of a man talking to Ira came from the closed room.

Ira screamed and the sound was a sound of pleasure. Ira was moaning in pleasure.

Sasha looked at Nikki in complete surprise.

"Don't look at me. You are the one who wanted the TV's sound low. Now enjoy the real show."

"Is this every day?"

"Well, almost. I would say. This girl is real horny!" Nikki raised the volume back again.

That sound had just come out of Ira's room. Sasha was even more confused. So, Ira had a boyfriend? Cool!

It was unlike in India where you have to hide and see each other. Sasha was a little shocked, but then she too had a boyfriend...

The TV's sound was loud, but Sasha could now hear all the sounds coming from Ira's bedroom. Sasha didn't know what to make out of this situation right now. A girl who drank like a fish was sitting next to her, and then there was another one in the other room having sex!

Chapter – 7

The city never disappoints; it's just so flawless. This was technically her new home, her new existence, and her new world. The sun was shining bright. It was 10:00 a.m. Sasha had gone to bed late, so she wanted to stay in her bed a little longer. Tired from last night? She was still thinking of the guy she had met at the coffee store… Rahul.

'Friends with benefits? Sounds such a good idea.' She talked to herself.

She lay under her warm sheets. She had no plans for the day. Where could she possibly go? She had no friends or family. The café was her place of work, and this was her home… At least for now. Having a roof over her head and having food on the table was a luxury! Rahul was a stranger, but she felt secure. He didn't look like a serial killer or anything like that.

He had dimples when he smiled and so did she. So, something was common. They would make cute babies if this went that far. She smiled again on her own.

She looked out of the window and the sky was clear.

The phone rang. She looked at the number and it was Rahul.

"Hello."

"Hey. It's Rahul. You slept well, babe?"

Sasha was shocked. She had just been thinking about him. Was this a sign?

"Yes. I slept well. I was just waking up."

"Ok great. I am glad I didn't wake you. So, what are your plans for today? Do you think you can go for a lunch?

"Mmm… yeah sure. It is my day off," Sasha was hesitant, but she dared to anticipate and see where this would lead.

"Sweet. Should I pick you up or would you like to meet me somewhere?"

"I think we can meet up somewhere. What time are we meeting, Rahul?"

"I think two is good for lunch? Not sure how your appetite would be by then?"

"Oh. That is perfect. I would be hungry." She took a pillow and put it under her arms as she sat up. The sound of this man was so sexy she wanted to stay on this phone call forever.

"Do you have a preference for dining, sweet?"

"Not really. I am ok with everything." Sasha was smiling. She loved how sophisticated this man sounded to her.

"Well then. Let's meet at Robson and we can decide where you would want to sit," Rahul told her.

"Ok. That sounds perfect. I will be there at 2:00 pm." Sasha was excited. A handsome man who spoke well and cared for her opinion? That was amazing.

Sasha was a little surprised. He was quite fast. She was not expecting him to call and ask her out on a date this fast.

'Oh, wait a sec. This is not a date,' Sasha tapped her hand on her forehead and smiled.

There was a happiness of some sort. She would finally have someone like a friend. She would know

61

this human in this unknown world. Her roommates were weird and she couldn't say it out loud. But now she had this new friend with benefits!

'Listening is also a part of it. It is a benefit.' She said to herself. Sasha was so happy.

'Oh God, such a good-looking guy is going to be my friend?' She jumped on the bed. She looked at the clock and it was almost 11:00 am. She needed to take a shower and get to Robson Street.

'Oh, what am I going to wear? I must not look sexy. We are just friends.' Sasha went to her closet and sorted through her clothes.

She took out jeans and a white T-shirt.

'This looks perfect. It doesn't look sexy or anything. Mmm… yeah. I am so happy.' She put the T-shirt against her chest, looked in the mirror and then twirled while she talked to herself.

It may sound crazy if someone heard Sasha talking to herself, but she continued. 'Let's go, Sasha. It's time to make some real friends in this new world.'

She grabbed her clothes and walked to the washroom. She dressed in jeans and a white T-shirt and got in front of the mirror. She put on a little eyeliner and a little lipstick.

'God, this is so much makeup.' Sasha was definitely trying to screw this up now. She was self-contradictory. Life was all about figuring things out as we go… This was exactly what Sasha was trying to do.

She had so many questions and no one to answer them.

She was all dressed up and ready. She wiped her red lipstick off and took a good look in the mirror.

'Let's go, Sasha, baby. It's time to make some good friends.' She grabbed her bag, got out of her apartment, and took the elevator. Living alone had taught her to talk to herself.

Sasha walked down the street. Now she had to figure out how to get to Robson Street. She was in no rush. It was just 12:30 p.m. on a Wednesday. She was excited to see the guy, but also liked to explore the city alone. She would have to learn to live in this new world eventually. You fall, and then there is only one way left. Rise.

If anyone saw Sasha right now, they would know she was in a good mood. She was happy… She put her headphones on as she left her apartment.

'Oh, what a sunny day,' she whispered to herself. The green trees, tall apartment building, almost spotless roads… you could sit on the sidewalk.

Sasha's mind was wandering just like she was alone in the city with a destination, but no rush to find it. It was 1:00 pm. Sasha must now start finding the destination. She put Robson Street on the search.

Google showed on the map twenty-five minutes by walk, and seven minutes by bus. Sasha went to the bus station and waited for the bus. She did not want to sweat after walking for nearly half an hour. She preferred to sit and observe the city. The bus arrived and Sasha hopped on to it.

"Hello," Sasha said to the bus driver.

"How are you today?" The bus driver responded.

"I am well, thank you," she replied taking the coins out of her purse.

She put coins in the meter and it gave her a ticket. She went ahead and took a seat. There was a wire hanging onto the sides above the windows.

People push that wire to let the driver know it's their stop next. The streets were busy. Sasha looked out of the window and she was smiling. The idea of friends with benefits was what was making her happy at this moment…

Life was difficult after her separation. She was left alone in this world where she knew no one.

But trying to figure life out, Sasha had almost forgotten her past.

Chapter – 8

"Hey, girl! Are you here yet?" Text from Rahul.

"Almost there," Sasha replied when her phone buzzed. She was on the bus, and her thoughts were all over the place. But the view from the city was a complete distraction. The sidewalks were full of people. Are people so well-dressed all the time? Sasha felt for a second that it was not a sidewalk but a ramp for models. The streets were clean. Then she noticed a police car and also that the police cars were parked and their lights were flashing. Sasha's bus took a little detour. She saw a man lying down, and he was handcuffed. Four policemen had surrounded him. The bus kept on going. This was how life was… You just keep driving as life gives you good scenes and bad!

Well, right now she was going to see some man she had just met.

Who and What exactly do you do when you are alone in the city and there is no one you can trust or rely on? If something is about to go wrong, no one is there to help you… and you take your chances. You rely on your gut feeling, faith, and a little hope! She had no clue what the benefits looked like.

Sasha looked out of the window and then looked at her phone. She was almost close to her destination. She must learn the streets slowly as she builds some friendships.

It was her destination; Robson Street. She pulled the wire to get off at the next station. The bus stopped and Sasha got off the bus.

"Thank you," she said.

"Have a good day," the driver responded.

"I am at Robson Street. Where should I meet you?" Sasha texted Rahul.

"You want to join me in a café? Or any special place you like?" Rahul texted her back.

"Café is great. Send me the address," Sasha replied.

"It's Doro's café. An Italian place. It's nice."

"Ok," she replied.

Sasha again put Doro's café on Google Search engine and found the address. It was just a block away. She started walking toward the café in a rush. Sasha was not paying any attention to any of the stores. She had a meeting and a guy friend to hang out with. Her heart was beating a little faster. Well, she was also walking fast!

'Oh, there he is. A handsome stud!' She whispered to herself.

Rahul was dressed in a white shirt and blue jeans. Sasha walked closer to him and noticed his well-built chest popping out of his shirt. She also noticed how sleek this haircut was. Sasha scanned his profile and his excellent physique and let out a sigh.

'Oh my! He is so good-looking!' She whispered to herself while rubbing her nose so Rahul could not see she was talking to herself.

"Hello," Sasha walked up to him and made eye contact.

"Oh, you made it. How are you?" Rahul spread his arms and gave her a warm hug. Sasha could feel his strong arms.

Sasha responded and hugged him back. It was not a tight hug, but a hug you would give to someone you had just met.

Instantly, that hug made her feel warm. She had been a little nervous before meeting him.

"Ok, let's go in. Unless you have some other place in your mind?" Rahul asked Sasha as they both stood outside that elegant café. People were waking by and the street was busy.

"Well… I don't know the street, so I wouldn't know any good place. I like coffee," Sasha clarified.

"Oh, ok. Sure, let's go into the café then," Rahul pushed open the door as Sasha walked into the café.

Sasha smiled again, this time not while looking at Rahul. How the hell was this man so good-looking and so sophisticated at the same time? Sasha gave him another glance and he appeared charming. He had dimples on his cheeks, and she could see his skin through his nicely trimmed beard.

'Oh, Lord! Hopefully, he doesn't see me checking him out.' She was so confused about this meeting. Sasha had no clue what was going on. She was lost in this new café, a handsome man, and the excitement of making a new friend.

This was not a date... Sasha told her head again. Who knows, he might have a girlfriend. Or he may even be married? Maybe kids? Sasha had no clue, but she was about to find out!

"Sasha. Is there something you prefer?" Rahul asked her.

"Caramel Macchiato and an apple pie," Sasha looked at the menu on the board.

Rahul placed the order.

"Here is your receipt. I will bring your order to the table..." The server was a blonde girl. and her hair was tied up in a messy bun. How do women look so beautiful all the time?

"Thanks, you," Rahul smiled at the blonde girl, and she smiled back at him, and then she noticed Sasha.

It wasn't just Sasha checking him out; the server was flirting with him too.

Well, he was not her boyfriend. They were just going to be friends with benefits.

They both took a table and sat opposite each other.

70

"So how are you? And thank you for coming out," Rahul put his phone aside and his wallet back in his pocket.

"I am ok. So, you are in real estate?" Sasha tried to put her hands on her legs. She rubbed her hands together and held them tightly. She didn't know how this meeting with a stranger would take place. She picked up the fork and fiddled with it.

"I am a real estate agent and have been in the industry for a few years. And how about you? Are you new in your job?"

Sasha was mesmerized by his manners. How professional he looked even on a day out with a girl.

"Yes… I just got this job and have been working there for a couple of months now."

What life had she lived before this? It was nothing but an illusion. Now she just wanted to fall in love with someone.

The day was gorgeous and she was with a very handsome man. Men are the most simplified creatures on the planet. They want to be taken care of and loved and in return, they give you all. But the men she had been meeting were not regular humans, but monsters. She was hoping Rahul wasn't one… A monster.

"Oh, nice. Where did you work before this?" Rahul tried to make conversation.

"Mm… well, I have not worked that much," Sasha told him with hesitation.

"Oh okay. That café is not a bad place," Rahul seemed unimpressed, but he tried not to show it. Sasha was just an ordinary girl working in a café.

"You probably have a lot of work, right?"

She was willing to learn if someone would teach her. She would take a job. The country was new and so were the people, but you had to take your chances and your calculated risks. Real estate? Sounded like a great venture for Sasha. She could possibly work with him. That was what she was thinking. Anyways, what did friends with benefits mean? He needed help, and she had time. It seemed to work for both of them. Sasha smiled.

"Yes. I do have a lot of work. I don't have a schedule. I work on my own time." Rahul's phone was on the table and he checked it every few minutes.

"Oh, nice. I can help you with paperwork sometimes?" Sasha sat comfortably on the chair, crossing her legs. She was a little nervous.

Just then the server brought their order. Sasha was nervous, but also tried to find out if she could work with this man.

"So, what were you saying?" Sasha took a sip out of her coffee…

"What were you asking?" Rahul took a bite out of his food.

"I was asking if I could help you sometimes if you have so much work. I can learn at the same time?"

"So yeah, sure you can help me with paperwork. Do you want to come to my place one day? We can have a drink or something?" Rahul took a sip out of his coffee and smiled at Sasha.

"Yes, that sounds like a good idea," Sasha innocently agreed to this proposal. What is the harm? She would not work in a café for the rest of her life… She was in a different world. She was the one who had to decide what was good or bad and she was the one who had to lead her life.

Her gut feeling was wrong, but she agreed to go to his place. The smile he had on his face didn't match the words he was saying. But do you have a choice? You always have a choice, but she was willing to take a risk. She was ready to dare... The need was more robust than the gut feelings right now. She would go over to his place. The day was still gorgeous. They both were laughing. Rahul? He was a charming man and successful.

Chapter – 9

Sasha pulled out her laptop from under her bed. She was alone in the apartment. It was still her day off. Her meeting with Rahul had been amazing. She could still imagine dimples in his cheeks and his long eyelashes. Even though they were supposed to be friends with benefits, she had a secret crush on him.

What do you do anyway? You are single and living alone in a new country where you know no one.

Sasha's idea of friends with benefits was to help him with his work as she could then learn real estate. Rahul was an opportunity.

Sasha logged onto her social media, **Instagram.** She wanted to find out all about Rahul. She looked at the business card he had given her and searched for his Instagram.

'Wow!' Sasha was sitting alone, and couldn't believe how hot this man looked in his photos.

Rahul's page was full of selfies. Most of his photos consisted of his selfies. Might be a little self-centered?

'Mm… why would he want to be friends with me?' Sasha scrolled down the page which was open to the public. He had many photos of his on the page, most of them in tuxedos.

She let out a sigh… This was so unreal. She was mesmerized by this man. In just two meetings, all she was thinking was him.

She scrolled down more and saw more photos of him with women.

'Oh, girls? Wow.' Sasha's eyes were glued to the computer. She wanted to search some more on him. She put his name in the search engine and found his Facebook.

She looked for more information. 'Oh, he is single and interested in women.' She had a broad smile on her face. She scrolled down and saw photos of him.

'Oh, I see. He likes to travel. Greece?' she continued to scroll down.

Just then, she heard a door open. She heard some sounds, but Sasha was so involved in discovering more about this new human in her life that she did not pay attention to who was in the apartment.

Sasha had to learn how to live alone. But not forever. She would need a companion eventually. She had these walls, her bed, and this window where she sat, dreamed, and longed to be with someone. All the relationships she had right now were shallow and business-related. Maybe she could open up to her new friend Rahul?

Sasha's window had a little sitting area. She had made her little world beautiful. She had a small TV on the wall. It was like living in a hotel before she made this small space hers. There was detail in every corner. Lavender branches were hanging onto her wall, the side table had her photo, and there were candles on the dresser. This wasn't just a place to sleep anymore. It was her space and she had fallen in love with it. The space that took you in no matter how the world is treating you. But she also wanted to be with someone she could call hers. Could Rahul be that one?

Sasha went back to the search engine and tried to find out more about this new guy Rahul in her life. She found his Instagram profile which was private.

'Oh, should I send him a request?' Sasha took a minute to think while she talked to herself.

'Mm… no, forget it. He will think I am desperate or something.' She closed the window and went back to his Facebook.

She heard a loud laugh. It was Ira. Sasha still paid no attention.

"Baby, let's go to your bedroom, or are you just going to keep teasing me like this here on the couch?" The sounds were clear coming through Sasha's bedroom walls. She had no music on, and the apartment was quiet, but not anymore.

"I don't want to go into the bedroom. I can't walk. You made me so drunk." Ira was sitting on this man's lap and her arms were around his neck.

He held her tightly, put his hands on her bra, and then unhooked it.

She took his hand out and got angry.

"Stop. I don't like this stuff." Ira tried to take his hands off her, but the man wasn't stopping. He lifted her dress, put his hand underneath, and touched her. Soon he was kissing her cleavage.

"Don't put your hand in there. I just met you." Ira could barely talk and was drooling.

"Well, I thought you liked me, and that's why you brought me here to your apartment. Yes?" He kissed her on the neck, sucked her skin, and left a blue mark. Ira was still struggling to get off his lap. But she had no balance, her feet were unsteady, and she was completely staggering and swaying.

He then put his hand under her dress again. This time Ira allowed him. Or she didn't have the strength to fight back. She was way too intoxicated to give this man a fight.

Sasha could hear the sounds and she also heard Ira trying to stop this man.

Now curious and worried, Sasha got up and tried to find out who Ira was with. Maybe she was getting raped? She opened her door and went to the kitchen.

"Hi," Sasha said to Ira.

"Hello," Ira replied while still in this man's arms and sitting on his lap.

Sasha was so confused. How come all of a sudden, she was all calm?

"She is my other roommate," Ira told the man who appeared to be in his late forties.

"Hello," the man greeted.

"Hi," Sasha made no gestures but said a cold 'Hi'. She had no clue what was going on.

She opened the fridge, took the water out, and poured it into the glass.

The man kept kissing Ira on her neck and held her tight in his arms. She looked like she was drunk. Sasha tried to avoid everything she was seeing, but it was so visible. Why didn't he care about her being in the room?

She had a good glance at Ira again. She was in a mini white colored dress and could barely hold herself straight. Sasha was disgusted with this whole situation. It was weird. She quickly went into her room and shut the door. She didn't want to be part of this.

Five minutes later she heard sounds of moaning and deep breaths. She heard Ira screaming almost.

She opened the door slightly to see what was happening and to her complete shock, she witnessed live sex in the living room.

The man's pants were down and she could see his bare back. Ira's white dress was still on, but her red-laced panties were on the floor. The man was on top of Ira and was pounding her on the couch. Sasha quickly closed the door. This was horrendous.

She had just witnessed Ira's legs hanging in the air and this strange man's buttocks and his pants halfway down to his knees.

'Oh, is she getting raped? Should I call the police?' Sasha who could not believe what she had just witnessed, wondered. She wanted to puke, but for that, she would have to go to the bathroom which was outside where two people were having sex.

She had never signed up for this stuff... Sasha put her headphones on and turned up the music to avoid the sounds that were coming from the living room. All of a sudden, her peace was taken away. Her room which was so peaceful seemed to be turned into chaos. After all, it's not the place that can bring peace to you. Peace comes from within, and she was feeling distorted from inside.

'Dear God, where did I get stuck? No wonder the rent was so cheap. One chick does the drugs and the other one just has sex in the living room.'

Feeling sick to her stomach, Sasha hid her face under the blanket and listened to music.

The man pulled his pants up. The stranger was about to leave the house. Ira lay on the couch and she was drunk. Her eyes were closed and her legs were hanging on the floor.

Sasha took her headphones off to see if she needed to call the cops. There was an intruder in the house and her roommate might be getting raped. Sasha got up and locked her door from inside. What if this man was a rapist? Just then she heard the click of the main door.

'Ughhh, finally he is gone. It's just 7 pm and the day is still bright.' Sasha got out of her bed and went to check up on Ira. What she saw made her even more sick. Ira's underwear was still on the floor. Sasha drew down her dress and pulled her legs up on the couch. She took the throw and covered up her body.

The apartment was silent; it was just Sasha and this drunk girl there.

'Poor Ira,' Sasha sighed and then poured water into a glass and left it next to Ira on the side table. She put her shoes on and went out the door. She needed some fresh air to clear her mind.

Chapter – 10

Sasha left the apartment and went and sat outside in the lobby. There was a little seating area with blue couches in the lobby. It was a high-end building located in the heart of downtown. The walls had beautiful modern art paintings and in the middle was a coffee table that had a large vase with tall yellow-colored flowers. The interior was vibrant and to enter this space, everyone needed a fob. There was also a marble-top reception desk, where a Caucasian man was always entering names or helping people out.

There was a large chandelier in the middle of the ceiling and a few large paintings on the walls. She couldn't believe she was able to rent a room in this building. She sat on a couch and noticed people walking by. She noticed most of the people in the building were Caucasians, but there a few Asians too. She had not seen any Indian in here. Oh yes... Vian was also an Indian, the man she had met near the garbage can. She forgot about Rahul. Well, Vian was also very handsome. A man is at his ultimate power when he is good-looking and has money, and a woman is at her ultimate power when she is beautiful and has nothing to lose!

Sasha still didn't want to go upstairs. What she had just witnessed was horrifying. The price for the room was low, but the price for her mental peace was being compromised. Sasha wanted to take a walk and get some fresh air, but her body refused to walk. So, she sat on one of the blue couches and watched people to distract her mind.

"Oh, hello, stranger." Just then a sound distracted her.

She snapped out of her thoughts and noticed Vian, the penthouse guy standing in front of her.

Wow, he was so handsome! She heaved a sigh. How weird it was that she was just thinking of him. But she would not tell him that. He would think she was hitting on him. Well, she should, but she would not.

"Oh hi." She fixed her hair and tried to hide that she was in her sweatpants and a T-shirt. Sasha didn't even realize she had left her apartment in a

T-shirt and sweatpants. She had no bra on and now a good-looking man was standing in front of her. She didn't know what to do.

"You are ok? You sitting here by yourself?" Vian was dressed in a pink cotton shirt and blue pants. He switched his bag onto the other shoulder.

Already confused, Sasha didn't know how to handle this awkward situation. What else could she do? She didn't know how to avoid this situation.

"I am ok. Thank you." Sasha fixed her T-shirt. In her head she had one thought… why did he always see her like this? Even though he seemed to be an out-of-her-league kind of guy? She had let her heart have a crush on him. You can have a crush on whoever you want. Brad Pitt or Imran Khan… It's not like you can get them.

"I just got off from work. You can come and relax at my place if you like?" A very sophisticated-looking man just invited Sasha into his space.

She hesitated for a bit, but then agreed… maybe she could vent to him? She needed someone to hear what had just happened. How else do you make friends? You have to trust someone. She had Vian and Rahul. But she also had a crush on both of them.

That didn't make her a slut, did it? She was allowed to have a crush...

"OK," Sasha put her flip-flops back on and followed Vian.

He smelled so good. Sasha took a long sniff as she followed him into the elevator. He was hot, but out of her league. In just two meetings, Sasha knew and could sense that Vian was a successful man. She had no chance here.

Also, she was divorced. There was a stain on her that couldn't be removed no matter how far she tried to run away from her past. They both got in the elevator and Vian pressed for the top floor. They both could hear each other breath.

"Do you have to go far to work?" Sasha broke the silence.

"Oh no. Just across the street. You see that building? That's where I work." Vian smiled at Sasha.

"That's nice. Otherwise, it takes so long to commute in Vancouver," Sasha crossed her arms to hide her no bra situation.

"True. The traffic is crazy in the evening. I feel blessed to work just across from my home."

The elevator opened and the corridor was huge. There were orchids in the corridor and a large painting. There was a double door. Vian swiped his fob and unlocked the door.

"Come on in, Sasha." Vian stepped in.

'He remembers my name?' She just then realized she had forgotten what his name was! Oops! Out of sight, out of mind.

Sasha walked into the house.

"Wow… you live in a palace?" She was stunned by the size of the place.

"Thank you," Vian smiled.

"What are you like, some sort of CEO?" She walked in.

Vian was quiet.

"You live in this huge place. This is like a mansion. I didn't know this building had this." Sasha walked in looking at the high ceiling, the like of which she had never seen before. It was like she was in some wonderland.

"You have to do all the household chores yourself? Looks like a lot of work cleaning this place?" Sasha questioned him innocently.

Vian smiled and put his bag on a table that seemed to be meant for his work bag. There was also an elegant wooden table with a hanger where he hung his jacket. He let Sasha talk. He listened to all she had to say. Sasha forgot her messy hair, the T-shirt she had worn, and a bra she hadn't worn.

A six-foot-tall Buddha statue was located right at the house's entrance. She walked a little further and saw a big block of rock and water flowing through it. The blue lights reflecting on this fall made it more elegant. The kitchen was open concept and had dark cabinets, black with silver fittings. There was an island in the middle with bar stools. The bar stools had red velvet covers and golden arms.

"Can I please take a tour of this place? It's stunning." Sasha almost forgot about her roommate Ira, as if she were in a wonderland.

"Yes, please go ahead. Be my guest. Would you like to have a drink?" Vian poured himself a glass of wine.

"OK," she agreed to a glass of wine.

Sasha walked around and was shocked by the sight of this place. It was huge. She looked out of the window and could see all the other windows; windows of other buildings. She could also see a hint of the sea. Then she looked down and could see the busy streets. The cars looked very tiny, like ants.

Vian walked up to Sasha standing by the window looking down at the streets, and passed her a glass of wine.

"You are rich," she said, taking the glass from him.

Vian laughed… "Sure, if you say so."

Vian sat on the arm of a couch, putting one leg over the other.

"And you have to still go all the way to the garbage cans and throw your stuff? You have no one to help you?" Sasha very innocently threw a question at him.

Vian couldn't stop laughing again while he stood at the bar staring at Sasha.

"Well, my housekeeper who lives here with me is on holiday. So, I have been doing everything by myself."

She had no makeup on. Sasha was walking around and looking at things like it was a museum of some sort.

"Your housekeeper lives here all day?" She again questioned Vian.

"Yes. He helps me out with cooking my food and organizing my house. Good thing he is on vacation, else we would have never met." He smiled and looked at Sasha.

"Oh, lucky guy. You know, if you want, I can be your housekeeper. I mean, it looks like a good deal. You live here in this big penthouse and clean and cook for just one and you make money on top of that." She took another sip and laughed.

"You have a great humorous personality, Sasha," Vian told her.

"Oh, you have no idea… what will happen if my mother sees this. She will probably make this housekeeper do double the work." Sasha just went on talking without any restraint.

"Where is your mother?" Vian looked at her face, ignoring the fact that she was in her sleepwear and was braless, even though he could see her nipples sticking out of her old ragged T-shirt.

"Oh, my parents are in India. I am the only one here in this strange world," Sasha smiled at this statement.

"Oh. So, you are a student, or on a work visa?" Vian questioned her.

"What, you are interviewing me or something?" She smiled again. Sasha knew she could never get this man. So, she could say whatever came to her mind… nothing would matter.

"No. Just asking."

"Well. I will tell you when we know each other well." She took another sip from the glass and picked up a strip of cheese from the tray in front of them.

"OK. Sure. I thought we knew each other. Since you are in my house?"

"You know. What was your name again?" Sasha took a sip out of her wine glass.

"Vian," he smiled and shook his head at her honesty. Vian ran a company of fifty employees. His schedule was busy, but he was with Sasha watching her every move. Sasha who had forgotten his name, just remembered Vian it was!

"So, Vian. You know I have never seen such a pretty house before. I mean, this Buddha? It is taking up space that is half of my bedroom. Wow. So, what do you do to make so much money?" Sasha still looked around while she talked to Vian. She was more focused on the interior and the house than on him.

Vian laughed again. "Sasha you are so funny. You just changed the topic. I am an Executive/Producer Director for international VFX at Siena Focus World."

"Oh, so complicated. I have no clue what you do, but it sounds very cool." Sasha had already finished her wine and placed the glass on the counter.

She went under the chandelier above the kitchen counter and gave it a closer look. "This looks like a big cluster of stars. You are so lucky. You don't have to go far to work, and you live here in this nice expensive place."

"Thank you, Sasha. Can I get you another glass of wine?"

Sasha opened the door and went onto the balcony. There was a lovely patio set in white décor. There was a built-in BBQ in one corner, and on the other corner, there was a waterfall with a purple LED light built in.

"Sure. I can have a glass of wine. I don't have to drive. You don't listen to music, Vian?" She handed him the wine glass that she had placed on the counter.

"Oh, I do. What sort of music are you into, Sasha?" Vian took her glass and waited for her answer.

"I like any music. But to be specific, seventies and nineties music." She looked down from the balcony and noticed how small everything appeared.

"I will be back with the wine and music of your choice. Unless you want a Margarita? I can maybe make you one?" Vian asked.

"Oh, Margarita? Sure, I can take one. I am definitely not dressed for a Margarita," she laughed.

"You look amazing to me. Let me get you some food and your choice of drink," Vian told her and went into the kitchen.

Sasha sat on the couch on the patio. Vian walked in with a glass of Margarita, and Nachos. He handed the drink to Sasha and placed the nachos on the table.

"Should I turn on the fire for you, gorgeous?" Vian took a seat and started sipping his glass of wine.

"Umm… Ok. Thank you. This Margarita looks amazing. Did you learn to make them somewhere?"

"I wasn't a bartender. It's just hit and miss," Vian smiled.

Sasha laughed at his joke. "Well, I didn't say that. I mean, you cook well and make good drinks, live in this house, seem pretty well off, and not a bad-looking man. And single? Why?" She asked.

"Well, haven't found the right one yet," Vian looked at Sasha and smiled.

"OK. Neighbor. I hope you find your girl soon." She drank more from her glass, took more food, and put it on her plate.

They were both quiet, and the music was on. Sasha sipped from her glass of Margarita and so did Vian. Sasha walked around and was still looking amazed by everything she was witnessing. This was like magic, as if she was in a fairytale.

"This is a beautiful garden," Sasha walked on the grass barefooted, staring at the lights hanging from the plants. A light wind was blowing, making her hair fall onto her face. She sipped on her Margarita and removed her hair from her face.

"Thank you, and so are you," Vian was leaning against the wall, praising this raw beauty standing in his house.

"You are so kind."

She was in a very rich house. She could easily be Vian's housekeeper, but then he was a man and she was a woman and they were both young and hot!

"Wow, you are rich! You must have lots of women after you if there is no girlfriend yet?" Sasha took the last sip from her wine glass and put it on the table in front of her.

Vian laughed at her comment again. "Can I get you another glass of a drink, Sasha? Let me make you a little more drunk. You sound funny."

"No, I should go. Thank you, though. You are really nice." She put her shoes back on.

"And you are so rich," she smiled. Sasha was buzzed as she said this and walked closer to the doors. She could barely walk straight.

"You know, this is what happens when you don't drink a lot. You get drunk in like two or three glasses of wine," she laughed again as she tried to hold herself.

"Well, thank you for visiting. Maybe if you like we can go for dinner and a movie one day?" Vian asked her.

"Oh, dinner and movie? Sounds like a good plan. But can we go somewhere where I can pay my own bill? You know I am not rich like you are," she looked at Vian.

"You are very funny, Sasha. Sure. How about you pick a place," he laughed.

"Ok, this sounds like a better idea. We can definitely do something that I like someday," she hugged him and got in the elevator.

"Thank you, Vian. Bye."

"Bye, Sasha. Take care."

The elevator doors closed and she pressed her floor number.

Chapter – 11

Sasha was back in her apartment. Ira was no longer there.

She looked out from her window and could see the city look alive. She could barely see anything from Vian's house. She could not believe what she just saw. So, there was a full house on top of this building? She was lost in her thoughts. Sasha had no clue there could be a house on top of the building with a balcony and a big fire pit. She was amazed at the mini garden in there. It was like she had walked into a dream. This room she was in felt so small. But hey… her view was better than what he had. She could see things and people walking on the streets.

Just then there was a knock on the door.

Sasha got up and opened the door and it was none other than Nikki.

"Hey girl, what are you doing alone in here? You want to smoke up?" Nikki was dressed in tights and a leopard print halter top. Her nails were painted pink and had little crystal art on each nail. Her ring finger nail had a bow art on it. She had her lips pumped and was wearing a thin silver necklace that had her name on it, "Nikki". Her eyelashes were long and thick. She was wearing a lip gloss. She had a brown-colored bag with LV and star logos on it.

Nikki opened the sliding door and walked out onto her balcony and Sasha followed her.

"So, what's new?" Nikki lighted her joint and smoked from it. Then she passed it on to Sasha.

"Not much. No, thank you," Sasha refused to smoke weed.

"What's wrong? This stuff should make you relax." Nikki took another Toke of smoke.

"Oh, I just had some wine," Sasha wanted to hide from her that she had been all alone with a man in his penthouse.

"With who?" Nikki was smoking.

"With a guy in our building who lives in a penthouse," Sasha hesitantly told her. She did not have a clue what her reaction would be. Being alone with a man is never a good idea.

"Oh, wine with the penthouse man? Oh… tell me more." Nikki smoked more and then she put her Doobie in a tube.

"Well. He was nice. I was sitting all alone in the lobby and he asked me if I wanted to join him. I didn't say no. He has a housekeeper who has a bigger room than ours." Sasha was still in shock when she gave her roommate all the details. Her eyes were wide open even without smoking weed.

"More. Tell me more. This is interesting. I have lived here for so many years and have never bumped into this man. Is he hot? What does he do for work?" Nikki poured wine into her glass and took a sip.

Sasha took out the card and read it and was in shock. Vian had given her the card and she had just put it in her pocket.

"EXECUTIVE PRODUCER/zzz… of Digital Film Productions," Sasha read the card and was shocked. She had been just drinking wine with some EXECUTIVE PRODUCER/DIRECTOR?

"Oh well, well… EXECUTIVE PRODUCER/ DIRECTOR? Married? Hot?" Nikki drank more wine.

"He is not married and also he is handsome," Sasha smiled.

"Ahh. Rich, single, and hot? Damn, girl! Looks like you just hit the jackpot."

"It's not like we are dating or going to date. I just met him, Nikki. I am not that lucky that someone like him would choose me. Maybe he was just bored and he had me over," Sasha told Nikki.

"Why do you say that? You are beautiful. Any man would want to be with you," said Nikki who was still drinking.

"No, Nikki. It's not as easy as you think. He is an EXECUTIVE PRODUCER/DIRECTOR and I am just a waitress," Sasha replied.

"Ahhh ahhh ahhh… sure. He just invited you for no reason?" Nikki laughed aloud.

"Seriously… Why don't you believe me? There is nothing, nor will there be anything," Sasha told her again with confidence. She knew she had a divorce tag on her and no one else needed to know that. She could probably never tell Vian about her divorce.

"Anyways. It's my birthday in a few weeks and we are taking a limo downtown. You want to come, Sasha?" Nikki asked Sasha.

Sasha had never been in a limo before. She had seen them in movies. She had no reason to be in a limousine. She saw an opportunity to have an experience in a limousine and party with the girls. She had partied with girls before, but that was in India. This city was new, people were new, and everything was different. Her eyes shone. But her mind had questions. How could she afford to go in a limo? It must be expensive? And what happens in a party like this? Sasha was curious. She was tempted... Tempted to see something she had never seen before.

"I am not sure," she replied in hesitation.

"Babe, Ira is planning this birthday for me. I will ask her to invite you too. Just come. Trust me, you will have a lot of fun," Nikki told her excitedly. Her eyes glowed.

Sasha had just had wine with some EXECUTIVE PRODUCER/DIRECTOR and now an invite to a party? She was tempted, but could she really go?

What was happening with her life? What had the universe to offer?

"Ok. Thank you." Sasha agreed to this deal with a smile on her face. She could always refuse if her heart said no.

"That will be so much fun. You, Ira, and I with my other friends. Oh, GOD! I can't wait."

Sasha had never seen Nikki not smoking or drinking. How could someone never be sober? What a life… It must be amazing to be so rich or to be born to rich parents.

High and drunk, Nikki turned up the music and danced in the middle of the living room. Sasha was watching her. Nikki took her hand and dragged her onto the floor with her. Now, they both were dancing. Sasha was hesitant, but then Nikki held her tight, brought her close, and put her arms around Sasha. Sasha held herself back and now they both rocked on the floor, hugging each other.

"You are my sister from another mister, Sasha. I love you," Nikki couldn't stand properly. Sasha held her tight and walked with her while she staggered and almost fell. Somehow, they both made it to her room.

Sasha tried hard to help her as she had also consumed a few beers and was intoxicated. Two drunk friends were trying to make it to the room. Sasha felt some real warmth when she was holding Nikki.

She put Nikki on her bed and covered her with a blanket.

"Lie down with me. I don't want to be alone," Nikki, who was drunk and stuttering, held Sasha's hand and made a request.

Sasha had no say. She went to the other side and slipped under Nikki's sheets.

Nikki put her arm around Sasha and laid her head on her shoulder! How warm it was. Sasha now had a friend whom she could call sister in this unknown world.

Aren't the feelings true when you are intoxicated? Or can you lie when your mind has been blocked? Sasha rested Nikki's head on her hand while she moved her hair off her face. Nikki was already sleeping…

Chapter – 12

The phone rang. It was 11:00 a.m. on a Friday.

Sasha got out of Nikki's bed and ran to the living room. Her head was hurting. She saw Ira in the kitchen cooking something.

RAHUL CALLING!

Sasha ignored the phone call. She went and took a seat on the couch.

"Good morning, Sasha. You want some pancakes? I am making some for myself." Ira took a bowl out and poured some flour into it.

Sasha had never really spoken to her before. It was a complete surprise for her that Ira was asking her if she wanted food.

Well, this is a good start! Sasha had been in this apartment with these women for a few months now and she had never seen Ira in the picture. She was never home. They saw each other and there was an exchange of hellos, but that was it. This was the first time Ira actually had a conversation with Sasha.

"Ok. I can have a pancake. Where is Nikki?" Sasha asks her innocently. She didn't want to be rude.

"She left an hour ago. She said she had work." Ira had a thick Indian accent. She was wearing pink colored pj's with the logo "Juicy Couture".

Her long hair was tied up in a bun. Sasha took a glass of water, went up to a couch, and sat in front of the TV.

A television show Keeping Up with Housewives, was on.

"Oh, I must have been in deep sleep. I didn't realize. When did she leave?" Sasha drank some more water.

"It's ok. You must have been tired." Ira put some pancakes on a plate and offered it to Sasha along with a syrup bottle.

"Thank you," Sasha took the plate and smiled at her. After all, she was not that bad, it seemed to her.

The scene with a middle-aged man in the living room was still haunting her. Maybe she had no one to talk to like Sasha? Who knows, maybe she was raped, but then she had heard moaning sounds coming from her room. Ira had huge eyelashes and her nails were very pointy and done up.

"You are from India," Sasha took the courage to ask.

"Yes, I am. I am on a student visa and have been here for over a year now," Ira cut some apples as she spoke.

Now Sasha was even more confused. How did this young lady transform herself this fast? She was branded head to toe. Sasha was trying to figure her out. Was she from a well-off Indian family? Just then Ira popped a question Sasha thought no one would ever ask.

"How about you? Are you from India? You have an accent like mine."

Sasha who had changed her name so no one would ever question her about her past, was taken aback. She didn't know what to say. Ira was a stranger. A lie would be a good idea.

"Oh, I am on a work permit," Sasha took a bite of the pancake and tried to swallow with water the lie she had just told this woman who she had seen may be getting raped in the living room they were both sitting in. Raped? Or not raped… Either way, it was not a scene she had ever thought she would have to encounter while living in an apartment.

How dark this room looked in the broad daylight right now, and how bright it was in the darkness of the night dancing away with Nikki while they both forgot the reality of life in their intoxicated state.

The only line that Sasha remembered from last night was, "You are my sister from another mister." Sasha smiled on her own. Those lines were in her mind.

Sasha gave another glance at Ira. Sasha noticed that she had a belly piercing. This made Sasha more curious. This roommate of hers was nothing but suspense.

Sasha broke the silence.

"You work somewhere?" Sasha took a bite from the pancakes.

Ira put a pot on a stove and started heating water.

"I am making tea. You want some?" Ira ignored Sasha's question and put some tea bags in the boiling water.

"Ok," Sasha was wondering how she was such a caring girl. Could she be an escort? Should she be judging her over her personal life? And who was she to judge her anyway?

"Nikki told me you are coming to the party. It's her birthday coming up soon. She said you will try. What is your plan?" Ira added some cardamoms to the boiling water… The whole room smelled like tea. Tea and pancakes were no great combination, but Sasha didn't care. She just went with the flow. Plus, food always tastes better when someone else is cooking.

"Yes, but I am not sure. She said she was taking a limousine. I have never been in any. Not sure if I can afford to go? It must be expensive," Sasha expressed her concern. Everything was new. Every day she had to figure out something. There was no one to tell her what was good or bad. It was just Sasha figuring out her life…

"You should come. There will be ten of us and the cost gets split among everyone. It's really like taking a bus around the town and you are safe for a little extra price," Ira explained and poured milk into the pot. She was making no eye contact with Sasha.

"Oh, ten girls? That is very nice. I like your pajamas," Sasha changed the conversation. She had no clue how expensive it would be. She could barely afford to pay her rent which was also cheap. But it takes time for a person to settle in the new world. And here she was all alone trying her best to restart her life all over again. Could she spend that money to party? She had to think.

"They are from Juicy Couture. I like them a lot too," Ira handed Sasha her cup of tea. "You should come to the party. It will be a lot of fun." Ira took her cup and sat down.

"Is there a dress code? Or can you wear anything?" Sasha picked up her glass of water and looked at Ira for an answer.

"You have never been in a club? No, you can't go in just anything. It isn't a Walmart. They won't allow you. So, dress to impress. Where have you been living for so long?" Ira questioned as she sipped her tea sitting next to Sasha on the same couch where Sasha had seen her naked and drunk under a man. Ira's hair was down and she had a petite body. Sasha noticed a tattoo on her arm. This was the first time in the many weeks she had been living in this apartment that Sasha was actually able to see this girl from so close. A belly piercing, a tattoo on her arm, and another one she noticed on her neck. Sasha shifted her focus away. She didn't want to creep on her.

Sasha was silent for a minute. Where had she been living? In search of a man in her past life, and later with a man who never wanted a woman to begin with. Sasha smiled. 'It was irony.' She wanted to say she had been married to a gay man who couldn't accept her as he was gay, but she held the thought. It was not that she was unwilling to share this with anyone. It was just irrelevant. It had no meaning to it. It was just a stain that was always dimming her shine. No matter how much she ran from it, it came back and haunted her at some time or the other.

"It's ok. I can help you out. Whenever you want. You can come and see my closet and borrow something." Ira took some food and put it on her plate distracting Sasha from her thoughts.

"Thank you, Ira. That is very kind of you, but I have to decide first. It really depends on my work schedule." Sasha had a thing on her mind. Could she be with these women? Everything seemed to be requiring a decision. The decisions were not small anymore, like what you will eat or what time you will sleep. Those were the decisions when she was a kid.

These decisions were big. She had to make her own money, pay her bills, and now had to decide if she wanted to go to this party.

These were really her decisions. Earlier someone else decided her fate, but this time it was she. She was the one leading her own life. Her decisions were the path to her future. And the time? It was the only commodity she had. Who she spent it with and how she spent it would decide where she landed in the future.

"It's really no big deal, Sasha. You will have lots of fun. Who knows, maybe you might find a boyfriend? You don't seem to have any," Ira smiled.

The phone rang. It was Rahul!

"Ok. I will come to the party. I have to take this call."

Sasha took her cup of tea and went into her room. She didn't want to tell anyone she was talking to this man. Rahul was not her boyfriend, but just an acquaintance. She liked him like a friend, but it might lead somewhere else, who knows?

"So, are you coming?" Rahul asked.

"Ok. We can meet at the café close to my place... Doro Café. See you there in half an hour?" Sasha questioned.

"No, babe. I want to go pub hopping. I will pick you up from your address. Text it to me," Rahul told her.

Like seriously? Sasha was thinking all of a sudden. Her gut feeling was saying no. But then she didn't want to let go of someone like him. She wanted to take some chances. It was indeed a calculated risk. But what could happen at the worst? He couldn't be a serial killer. Sasha had to make some friends. She knew no one. She had two roommates she knew, but needed someone to rely on.

Sasha hesitated and then agreed....

Sasha hung up the phone.

Life finally seemed to be happening. A new friend with benefits and then a party in a limousine?

All of a sudden Sasha's life was flooded with people. Vian, Ira, Nikki, and Rahul. She was smiling as she texted Rahul her apartment's address.

She took a dress out of her closet and changed. She selected a pair of white shoes to go with a red floral dress.

Sasha opened her computer and looked up Rahul's Facebook. She was looking for more things to know about him as she waited for her most recently added friend.

Chapter – 13

I AM HERE!

Sasha checked her phone and there was a text from Rahul. She was ready for her adventure with this man who wanted to be friends with benefits with her. She took the elevator and went down to the ground floor.

Rahul was waiting for her in his black Audi. His car's windows were tinted. Sasha had just met him once and now she was about to get into his car. You have to take some chances, she told herself.

Rahul was dressed in a navy blue suit with a gray shirt underneath. He had a nice tie on and Black Shades. He got out of his car and opened the door for Sasha.

"Thank you," Sasha smiled. No man has opened a door for her in the past. She had just seen this in movies. She checked the details and was quite impressed. She was nervous earlier, but now she felt great. How can such a sophisticated man do anything wrong to her?

"So? Where are we going?" Sasha got in the car.

"Well! There is no plan as such. Do you drink?" Rahul asked as he scanned Sasha from head to toe.

"I do."

And there it was, her first "I Do". Sasha noticed him scanning her. She smiled.

"Well, let's do a happy hour pub hopping?" Rahul asked her again as he drove out.

"Pub Hopping? Well, I have not done that before." Sasha looked at him and then at the beautiful day and the gorgeous street. The flowers were now in full bloom. She was slowly blooming.

The music was on and the car was moving slowly. Rahul and Sasha were chatting. Rahul, who had just got off from work, was telling Sasha about his new client. They both had something in common; they had met a lot of strangers every day during the last week.

"I enjoy dealing with clients. Every day is a new day. I just sold a property," Rahul said, looking straight ahead.

"I enjoy my work too. It is always a new day and new people. Some days there are grumpy people, but I am used to it now." She smiled as she scanned Rahul while he was looking at the road. Rahul's hair was cut nicely and there was a line on the side, where his hair was faded. Sasha reminded herself they were just friends… She shouldn't think any further.

"There is always a first time for everything, right?" Rahul parked his car on the side of the street and they both got out of the car.

Downtown was busy. There were people everywhere. All dressed up. Sasha was fascinated. Rahul was one of all these well-dressed people. And he had made time to see her. She was loving this new friendship. Plus, he didn't take her to a room or anything. They were about to hang out and maybe get drunk?

They both walked up to the pub by the water and took a seat at the bar. The view outside the window was the ocean. Sasha was with her new friend, in a pub by the water. All three things were so perfect.

"It's funny they have a happy hour," Sasha started the conversation.

"What is funny about it?" Rahul questioned as he smiled.

"You know? Lots of people are usually still working?"

"Yaa. So?"

"And they made this hour a happy hour? Where you can drink? And then you must go back to work?" Sasha raised her eye.

Sasha was looking at Rahul's long eyelashes. He was very handsome, but this was not a date. They were just two friends hanging out together. Plus, it was challenging for her to explain to anyone her divorce situation. She had almost forgotten about it, but it haunted her every time she thought of finding another man.

"Well one or two drinks are ok, no? People take a break from work and chill for a bit. It's no big deal. I do it all the time when I meet potential clients or buyers for the properties," Rahul said as he and Sasha sipped the beer.

Sasha smiled. She was enjoying the beer.

"So, tell me about yourself. You already know me."

"Well, I am Sasha, and I work at the café. I am from India and now I live here with two other girls as roommates," Sasha said, completely hiding her story. He was still not that close. She did not have to go into details. Plus, this was just the second time they both were hanging out. Maybe three meetings in total?

"Well, your English is great. You have a very British accent," Rahul looked into her eyes.

"Thank you," Sasha still tried to hide as much as she could. He was a friend, but not her best friend. She couldn't trust anyone this easily. They both sipped their drinks.

"So, this was our first pub of the day. Let us go to the next pub after we finish this drink, and we do this for the next two hours?"

Sasha nodded her head in agreement. What choice did she have anyway? It was not like she knew the city or knew what to do. She was seeing things, but this time the perspective was free and wild. She had no one to answer to!

They hopped from pub to pub for the next two hours checking out different pubs. Sasha was loving every bit of it. She was seeing different pubs and a lot of people. It was one beautiful afternoon. Something she was not expecting. She thought Rahul would discuss work with her, but this was different. They both were actually having fun. There was laughter and they giggled over the silliest things.

"Hey, Sasha… I am drunk, babe. How are you doing?"

"I can't walk anymore… I am going to fall."

"Oh, there is Chapters, a bookstore. Let's go there and look at books and we can sit down for a bit."

"Ok." Sasha followed Rahul… They both were drunk and they entered a beautiful bookstore.

"Let's go to the travel section." Rahul went to the travel section and sat on the floor with a few books.

"Ok. Sure." Sasha agreed to everything. When you meet someone, someone new, and you get to know them, that in itself is like reading a book. Rahul was Sasha's book right now. She was enjoying the company of this handsome man thoroughly.

Sasha could barely hold herself together. She had had a few drinks and was feeling a little tipsy. She sat next to him and leaned her head on Rahul's shoulder.

It was only Rahul talking.

"Look at this map. The world is so big," Rahul was looking in the book, but Sasha was looking at his eyes. There was something about his eyes. His beautiful long eyelashes? Sasha was loving this time. Just sitting and leaning on this new friend who she had just met.

"Where do you want to go if you get a chance to travel, Sasha?"

"Umm… I would want to travel to France and visit Paris," she smiled.

"Oh, very specific. Any reason why?"

"Well… It's pretty, and I wanted to see the Eiffel Tower."

"That's cool. And anywhere else?"

Sasha wanted to visit India and see her parents, but everyone was angry with her. Who would understand her there? No one. That was her home. Home is where everyone understands you and accepts you for who you are. Right now, she had no home. She did not belong anywhere. But she felt warmth sitting next to this stranger whom she had just met a while ago. Sasha felt safe and secure sitting next to Rahul. Then she responded…

"Maybe Vegas?"

"Oh, party girl! Speaking of parties, you want to come over to my place one day and we can hang out?"

There was silence for a moment. Sasha didn't say anything…

"Well… we already hung out? It will be fun if you come over." Rahul put his hands through his hair and smiled. His eyes were shiny and he looked straight into Sasha's eyes.

"Ok," she agreed.

Now he had a wide smile on his face.

Rahul started flipping through the travel books and told Sasha about the places he wanted to travel to, and those where he had traveled. Time was flying, but neither of them was looking at the clock. The store was beautiful and people were walking by. No one questioned these two drunk souls. It was for Sasha a really happy hour with her new very handsome friend... And she was already loving the benefits.

Chapter – 14

Sasha took a taxi back. She was a little sober as she walked into her apartment. Ira was still there. Sasha could hear her voice. She was on the phone with someone.

"YOU ASS HOLE. DON'T CALL ME EVER AGAIN."

Silence.

"WHERE DID THIS WIFE COME FROM?"

Silence.

"NO. YOU AGREED YOU WOULD GIVE ME 5K, AND NOW YOU ARE SAYING NO?

YOU USED ME FOR MONTHS... WE MADE THIS DEAL!"

Ira threw the phone on her bed.

She was fuming. Sasha saw her walking back and forth in her room. Sasha had never seen Ira's bedroom. But she gathered some courage to peek through her door which was a little open and she could hear this conversation. She could hear Ira's high-pitched voice. She could tell she was upset. She was still a stranger to her. Stranger enough to interfere right now. But Sasha didn't stop… they were roommates and they were here for each other….

"Sorry, but are you ok?" Sasha dared to ask.

"Oh hey. I didn't know you were here. Come on in," Ira fixed her hair and straightened her dress.

Sasha stepped in. Her room was pretty nice. It was not like her own room where she had no bed, but just a mattress, and a bunch of suitcases, and a window with white colored blinds. The only best part of her room was the window. It gave her hope and wings to fly over the city in her imagination. It felt like at times you were floating over the galaxy. The city lights were spectacular.

But Ira's room had lights of her own. Her room was very beautiful. The walls were colored beige. Her bed was of a wooden frame and had a nice floral comforter with a matching pillow set. She also had a closet that was not closed fully and Sasha could see some of her clothes hanging in there. Wow, so many, and just underneath was her shoe rack, and on the shoe rack were her heels all lined up.

"Wow… your room is so beautiful and you have so many clothes! You are so organized!" Sasha sat on a tiny chair that was placed in one corner. Sasha was surprised at how elegant this room was. Like it was not part of the apartment. The windows in the room had large-sized blinds and see-through floral drapes. Sasha looked through the blinds. The view was all buildings as far as she could see. It was creepy. You had to leave your window closed all the time. 'Who knows who can see you? Yes, those buildings are quite distant, but there are also binoculars too.' Sasha was having these thoughts in her head. She admired her own window way too much now. She had a nice view. It was a small room, but had a great view.

"Thanks," Ira said.

"It's like this room is not part of this apartment. It's so clean," Sasha was still stunned. "How do you manage to make this room look so pretty? Where do you find all the time between school and work?" Sasha questioned innocently. She wasn't sure if she was being rude, but she questioned anyway.

"Oh, I just like to make it look pretty. Nothing special. When you like something, you make time for it," Ira said in a thick accent. Sasha could notice hesitation in her voice, and did not make eye contact.

"Where do you get all this stuff from?" Sasha asked again.

"Well, most of the stuff is from spring cleaning. People leave their stuff out, and I pick it up," Ira still didn't make eye contact and casually told Sasha.

"Oh yes. Spring cleaning. I know. People sometimes leave such nice stuff out. I was so confused when I first saw it," Sasha smiled.

"Well, have you decided if you were going to party with us this weekend?" Ira questioned Sasha. Sasha was on the chair, and Ira was lying on her bed looking at Sasha.

"I think I can make it. My shift ends at 4 pm," Sasha had made her decision. She could have said no, but she was curious. Also, party with girls in a limousine? It sounded like a lot of fun. Sasha was tempted the minute she heard.

"Well then, you have plenty of time to dress up. You have a dress? We will leave around 8 pm." Ira got up and opened her closet. It was a small closet, but the dresses were hung tightly together.

"No. I have not got myself anything. I didn't have time to go shop as I wasn't sure if I could make it or not," Sasha explained.

"You can borrow from me. I have lots of dresses and you can keep the one you will wear for the party," Ira took out some dresses and laid them down on her queen-size bed.

"You can try them on. If anything fits and looks good, you can take it," Ira again told Sasha.

"Oh. Are you sure?" Sasha was still skeptical about everything Ira was saying. But who was she to judge? She needed to put her life together first.

"I don't see why not. We can have a mini fashion show if you like. You can try some on."

Sasha was thrilled. She took a dress and put it on. The room was not big, but Ira had a tall mirror to help her dress up. There were a few purses lined up on the top shelf.

"Wow. You look so beautiful, Sasha."

"Thank you," Sasha blushed.

"How do you have so many things, Ira, like shoes and dresses? You must be from a rich family in India?" Sasha turned around and looked into Ira's eyes. Ira focused on finding her a dress.

"Nope. I am just a regular office clerk's daughter. No richness here. But you can always make yourself into something, turn yourself into something. It's one life and you choose what you want to be and how you want to live. Here, try this one on," Ira passed Sasha another dress.

Sasha was more than confused. How could Ira be on a student visa and have all this? A nicely decorated, well-furnished room with expensive things… even a Louis Vuitton bag?

Sasha could never imagine owning an LV bag. Something she had discovered while working in the café. Who spends that much money on a bag? Might as well get something made of gold.

Sasha put another dress on… It was white, a bodycon dress with full sleeves. She was looking at Ira's closet. The furniture you can probably pick up off the street, but LV bag? She could not understand this mysterious girl, Ira. But she wanted to know how she did all this. How could she afford an expensive lifestyle and was still just a student? Then, that man in the living room having sex with her was also haunting her. What was this girl? Was she like an escort? All these thoughts were running through her mind, but she kept quiet.

"Oh, look at that… This dress looks so perfect on you. Try these heels on and we can do some makeup," Ira tossed some shoes toward Sasha.

Sasha wanted to forget that scene she had seen in the living room, but it was haunting her. However, Ira was just being nice to her. Was it because she was trying to hide something? Usually, people want to hide their darkness underneath something beautiful. But right now? Sasha was watching Ira help her with the dress.

Sasha picked up a dress and put it on.

"Oh, this looks great on you. Try a couple more on," Ira tossed a couple more dresses.

"Close your eyes," Sasha asked Ira.

"It's just me. Just go ahead and change," Ira casually told Sasha.

Sasha was hesitant, but she took her clothes off and tried the dress on. She could see that both Ira and she were of the same size. Both of them were petite. Ira however, had lighter skin. She was also wearing a lot more gold than Sasha.

"Yes. This looks great too. Let's do your hair and makeup." Ira took out her curling iron and her makeup. She put fake lashes on Sasha and then did her hair. Sasha sat there quietly and let Ira do the work.

"All right, Sasha. Put the heels on and let's go check yourself in the mirror," Ira told Sasha as she passed her the heels. They both went into the living room, where there was a full mirror by the entrance door.

Sasha looked at herself in the mirror and stood there for a second looking at herself and these 360-degree makeovers she had.

What could she say? She was speechless... Looking at herself in the mirror and at this girl Ira...

But they both were smiling and that's what mattered at that moment. Nothing else but freedom.

Chapter – 14

The café was loud. The front door was opening and closing. The air conditioning was keeping Sasha from sweating. There was a flood of people in the café. Patrick was running around, but Sasha was calm. She had seen more people than this in Indian restaurants. India was full of humans. You were never left alone. No matter where you were, there were people. Even in your own house. You would never find a quiet place. There was always someone visiting. There was a trail of thoughts in her mind.

"What can I get you?" Sasha was back in the café. She had left her hair curled and put it into a messy bun. Sasha was looking forward to the party with the girls. She couldn't stop thinking about it. She smiled and questioned the customer. But really she was happy she had a party to go to.

"One sweet cream nitro cold brew please," the customer said.

"That's all?"

"Yes. Thank you."

"You can tap or insert the card and your order should be ready to the left."

Sasha's phone buzzed in her apron's pocket.

She quickly checked it while the customers paid. It was Rahul's text.

'You want to come over to my place after work?' – (text)

She didn't respond. She was busy. She was however tempted. A man was inviting her to his place. Sasha's heart started to beat fast. But why? They were just good friends, right? With benefits. They had just met a couple of times, but she liked it. They could be good friends. She took her phone out and texted him back.

'What time?' (Text)

'When do you get off?' (Text)

'5 pm.' – (Text)

'Ok. Cool. Sending you the address… come whenever you get off.' – (Text)

'Ok.' (Text)

'Apartment – 24, Floor – 6, 1289, Hornby Street. My buzzer is 37.' – (Text)

Sasha looked at her phone and put it back.

The café started to slow down. It was past the lunch hour. Sasha had butterflies in her stomach. Even though she had agreed to go to Rahul's house, something didn't feel right.

Both Patrick and Sasha worked to clean up the mess. She took the broom and swept the floor. Her mind was racing even faster. She didn't know if she was excited or scared to go alone to someone's house. Well, it was an apartment in a building. There is nothing to be scared of, she told her mind. And Mounties were not like the police in India. These guys were more professional. Did she feel safe in India around the cops?

Not really! Sasha had heard horrible stories about the Indian police. You could bribe them and get away with murder. She had seen many times, people getting away from traffic violation tickets. How would you or can you trust police that can be bribed? Sasha tried to give herself all the reasons to convince herself that she was safe with this man. She was working, but her mind was not there.

"Almost time to go," Patrick whispered to Sasha in her ears.

"Oh. You scared me, Patrick," Sasha snapped out of her reverie as she dropped an empty glass.

"Oh, I am sorry, babe. I didn't mean to scare you," Patrick picked up the broken glass. There were no customers. The café had slowed down for a bit.

"No, no. It's ok. I was just in my thoughts." Sasha helped him. Sasha was contemplating if she should tell Patrick where she was going. Maybe if something happened? There would be someone who would know where she was, or he may just forget it. Sasha had so much on her mind. What if that man was a serial killer? She shook her head... No, he was a real estate agent. She decided not to tell anyone anything about this. She could handle a man alone if he misbehaved. Or was she just paranoid?

The time was moving fast, and before she e realized it was 5 o'clock.

Sasha took her apron off and fixed her jeans and T-shirt. She lifted her armpits and they were smelly.

But Rahul was not her boyfriend, so it didn't even matter.

'Bye, Patrick. See you tomorrow."

Sasha didn't tell anyone where she was headed to. It was a friend's house, not some stranger's. She must take some risks in life. Now when she was all on her own. She liked Rahul, he was warm. Sasha was comfortable around him. Maybe one day there could be something between them? He seemed pleasant and successful, educated, and well-mannered. She would have to find a boyfriend one day anyway. She walked out of her café and hopped onto a bus.

The bus was full of people during the rush hour. She was able to get a seat, but a lot of other people were standing. She looked out of the window and focused on the road. She had to get something for Rahul. You don't go empty-handed to someone's house for the first time. If this was India, she would go with a box of sweets, but in this case? She thought wine would be a better idea. She had heard when people went to house parties, they took wine or some sort of alcohol. There is an outer world and then there is a world inside you. Sitting on the bus and looking out of the window, Sasha paid attention to no one. How can you be in some other world on a bus full of people and not notice a single human? Well, she had Rahul on her mind right now. Sasha didn't have to tell anyone where she was going. There was no one she had to answer to. This is how freedom feels like. She smiled. Life seemed to be building. She had now Patrick, Ira, Nikki, and Vian, and Rahul was also going to be her friend with benefits.

The bus had reached her station. Her heart was beating fast. She took a sip of water and told her heart it would all be ok. He was a good friend. A friend with benefits!

She got off and walked on the sidewalk. She walked up to a liquor store and grabbed a bottle of wine. The road had lots of tall buildings and the added green plants across the road made this walk pleasant on a sunny day. Sasha reached the building and walked up to the buzzer machine.

She pressed buzzer 37. "HELLO!" The voice from the other side.

"HELLO. IT'S SASHA. I AM HERE."

"OH, HELLO, SASHA. COME UP. TAKE THE ELEVATOR TO FLOOR 6 AND I AM IN APARTMENT 24. WALK TO THE LEFT."

"OK."

Sasha followed the instructions. After she entered the building, Sasha got into an elevator. The elevator had mirrors. She looked at herself. She was looking ok. But she was not here to seduce a man. She was just going to hang out and then take off. She reached floor 6 and walked toward apartment 24. She stood outside the door of 24 and fixed her hair and T-shirt one more time before she rang the doorbell.

Rahul opened the door!

"Hey. You made it. I am glad you didn't bail out at the last minute," Rahul hugged Sasha and walked her into his apartment.

"This is for you," Sasha handed Rahul a bag with the wine bottle in it.

"What is this?" Rahul opened the bag.

"Little gift."

"Oh, sweety, you didn't have to do that, but thank you." He gave her another hug.

"Well, this is my first time at your place. So, it would have been rude to walk in empty-handed." She smiled. She was also gazing at Rahul who was dressed in a white shirt and black shorts. His top two buttons were undone and she could see his chest that was shaved. Sasha's heart rate went up a little. She was in a stranger's house. Crossing her fingers and hoping nothing would happen. Rahul was very handsome.

The apartment was spotless, she noticed. Like no one was living there. Leather couches and an ottoman in the middle. A big 70-inch TV had pride of place in the front. There was a solid wood dining table next to it and an open kitchen which was also spotless. She saw two doors and they were closed. She went ahead and took a seat on a comfy leather couch.

"Would you like a drink?" Rahul took a glass out and poured himself a scotch.

Sasha was nervous and her mouth was drying. She answered, "Sure. A glass of wine should be ok." What she wanted was a glass of water.

"Actually, can I also get a glass of water?"

Rahul opened a cabinet in his living room that Sasha noticed was full of different alcoholic bottles. Most of them were open and had been used partially. It looked like either he drank a lot or he had many parties.

"Can I add ice for you? Sorry, it's not chilled," Rahul asked as he poured some wine into a glass.

"No, it's fine. I can have it as it is," Sasha stuck her hand out.

"Ok. How about I cook you something? You hungry?" Rahul opened his fridge to see what was there.

Sasha was already feeling good about this night. He would cook something for her? A man who could cook? A handsome man with a career? Living in a "clean" apartment and could cook? That was a great resume if he would have been on a dating site. Who knows, maybe he was?

Sasha was impressed. What was the dark side to this? Nothing can be this perfect. Sasha was curious to know him.

"Ok. Sure."

Rahul opened the fridge.

"I have some Bell Peppers and some Perogies! Would you like that, Sasha?"

Sasha didn't know what Perogies were, but she was willing to try. "OK. Sure."

She got up and went into the kitchen to watch Rahul cook!

Sasha sat there and watched this man. Rahul took a remote and turned the music on.

"Do you have a music preference I could play for you?" Rahul looked at Sasha, who was sipping on her wine.

"I listen to all sorts of music. You can put on anything you like," Sasha was still looking at his place.

"Ahh, smart. You know you can tell a lot about a person from the type of music they listen to and the literature they read." Rahul took a chopping board out.

"Here we go." Rahul put roasted Bell Peppers on the plate with Perogies and gave it to Sasha.

"These smell and look yummy," Sasha said, taking the first bite.

"This tastes so amazing… Mm…" She didn't know what the best part of the meal was. That she was hungry? Or that it was Rahul who made the dinner? Or that it was tasty?

"This is like plain Indian samosa," Sasha said, taking a bite of the Perogies.

"You've never had them?" Rahul also brought his plate and sat next to her.

"No. Have never tried them before, but they are tasty." Sasha had come straight from work, and was hungry. The wine was making her tipsy as she was also tired from working all day.

"Wow. I am glad you like them. Sorry, I could have done better. I can make steak next time."

Chapter – 16

The evening was going great so far and was comfortable. Tired from work? The alcohol gave her a buzz a little faster.

Rahul poured more wine into Sasha's glass. She did not say no. She was certainly amazed by this man's hospitality. She could see tiny hair on his chest as he bent over to pour the wine.

But this was not a date. They were just two friends hanging out.

"You want to watch a movie, Sasha?"

"Sure. What sort of movie?"

"Anything you like?"

"Can we watch something from Bollywood?"

"OK. Sure, I can put some Bollywood movies on. I like old films. That works for you?" Rahul took the dishes and put them away. He got a glass and poured some vodka and some dry vermouth and added some ice and olives.

He took his phone and searched for a film that was on and gave Sasha a glass of martini.

"Oh. I can't drink this. I am already buzzed, Rahul. I had too much wine."

"Come on, babe… It's just one drink. I made it for you," Rahul looked into her eyes. Sasha didn't want to disappoint him. She took the glass off his hands, and without any further questions, she started sipping on it. It was his house, and he was just being nice. Rahul turned the music off and took a seat on the couch next to Sasha. He searched on the TV and put a movie on. They sat on the couch quietly and looked at the screen as they finished their drinks. Sasha put the glass on the table, but her hands were shaking. She could barely sit straight.

Rahul grabbed a bottle of tequila and two shot glasses and sat beside Sasha on the couch.

"Let's watch the old Sholay. What do you think?" Rahul made a suggestion.

"Sure. That is a good idea. We can time travel and go back in time," she slurred a bit and wiped her lips without him noticing.

143

They both sat there quietly and watched the film.

Sasha couldn't hold her head straight anymore, so she rested her head on Rahul's shoulder. The movie was on and there was silence. The only sounds in the room were from the movie. Sasha was now drunk and tired at the same time. She had no energy or strength. She wished she could pass out on Rahul's couch. But she couldn't. That would be so rude.

"You do this a lot?" Sasha broke the silence.

"Do what?" Rahul looked at her as he lowered the TV volume.

"Make girls drunk in your apartment?" Sasha smiled as she asked him the question.

Rahul laughed. "Not really. You are drunk?" He asked her.

"Sort of," she looks at him with a smile.

Rahul poured two shots and passed it to Sasha.

"No. I can't. I am already drunk. I don't think I can walk myself home if I needed to," Sasha refused.

"Come on, babe. Just one for me. I will drop you off later," Rahul insisted on Sasha taking another shot.

"I will throw up, Rahul," she told him as she held his arm. Sasha couldn't keep her head straight anymore.

"You will be just fine, baby girl," Rahul assured her.

She took a shot and put the glass down.

Rahul picked up the remote and raised the volume.

He then came close to Sasha and put his arm around her. Sasha let him. She was drunk and couldn't really think of anything. She had come back straight from work and was also tired. She wanted to sleep… but it was not her apartment.

Rahul moved her hair away from her face and let her lean onto his shoulder. He rubbed her shoulders and tried to kiss her. Sasha kissed him back on his lips. Just then she realized they were supposed to be just friends. She hesitantly pushed Rahul away and took his hand off her shoulder gently.

"Oh, I am sorry… I am just drunk and you are so beautiful," Rahul moved back.

"No, it's ok. I am drunk too," Sasha tried to fix her shirt.

"Babe. You want to see the rest of my house?" Rahul questioned Sasha.

"Oh yes. For sure. But we are in the middle of the movie. Also, I don't think I can walk," Sasha tried to be honest.

"It's a three hours long movie. Who cares. Let's go. Let me show you my castle." He stuck his hand out for her. Sasha held his hand and managed to get up from the couch. She could barely walk. She had had two glasses of wine, a martini, and a few shots of tequila.

Rahul held her and walked her to his office space in a den. "This is my office."

The office had a desk beside the window and a computer on a desk with a faux leather chair. She sat on the chair and spun around!

"Very comfy." Sasha spun the chair again as she laughed.

"It is indeed." Rahul leaned against the door looking at Sasha. His arms were crossed. His head was a little tilted and he was smiling. The walls of the room were painted light brown. On the other side of the wall, she noticed three frames hanging. A beautiful and positive wall art.

146

"Who decorated your place? It is so beautiful." Sasha looked at his nice and clean computer table. How could someone be this perfect? Rahul dressed well, had a clean house, had a great job, and he also made some food for her. Even if it wasn't of chef quality, at least he had put a meal together.

"Well, I did most of it, and some of it came as it is. Like wall colors and such," Rahul smiled, still standing leaning against the wall.

"You know those buildings outside? They look like tall lamps standing outside your window with all the lights turned on," she went up to the window.

"Ah… very nice thought. I never looked outside like that before," Rahul smiled as he walked up to her.

"I am sorry. I make no sense right now. I am very intoxicated with all that we drank. Thank you for a fun night. I am really enjoying this."

"Oh, I am glad you are!" Rahul held Sasha by her shoulders and raised her from the chair.

"Ok… let's go see my bedroom."

Sasha got up and sat right back again.

"I want to spin on the chair some more," she insisted.

"Babe… let's go. Don't you have to go home too?" Rahul told Sasha as he tried to make her stand again.

"Can I use a washroom?" Sasha asked him as she got up.

"Sure," Rahul walked her to the washroom.

She went into the washroom and noticed a frame with a Baywatch woman naked in the frame. She sat on the toilet and noticed another naked woman on the wall. She was drunk, but smiled. 'Now this looks like a bachelor's house. Naked woman on the walls.' Sasha laughed. There was no toilet paper. She got up and looked under the sink and in the drawers. She saw a set of condoms and wipes along with the toilet paper.

Had she seen this before getting drunk, she would not have had so many drinks. But right now, there was nothing she could do. Sasha shut the drawers and crossed her fingers, praying that nothing wrong would happen. Sasha held on to the walls and walked out of the washroom. She tried to walk straight.

"Oh, hey babe. You are okay?" Rahul held Sasha.

"Yes. I am ok," Sasha didn't question anything. She just followed him.

Chapter – 17

The night was going just fine. Sasha was completely mesmerized by this man. He could be a potential lover. Rahul had everything a girl would want in her man. He was very handsome, he looked very successful, a clean apartment meant he was very organized, and on top of all this? He could cook? A man who can cook and is good-looking? Sasha was absolutely in love with this evening. She wished it would never end. She was drunk and following this handsome beast around in his house. There were no red flags. Rahul was a charming man.

Sasha walked with Rahul, who was trying to hold her close to him. But Sasha left his hands and held on to the wall as she walked. The apartment was not that big, but right now, it felt like it was massive. Her body weight felt like it had doubled suddenly and she had to drag herself to his bedroom.

Rahul and Sasha walked to his bedroom. There was a queen-size bed that had a leather and solid wood headboard. There was a set of pillows nicely placed in bigger to smaller order. The bed was properly made. There was not a single wrinkle on the comforter. A painting hanging on a wall was a naked woman's portrait. A lady was lying naked on the grass and her breasts were visible. Sasha tried to ignore the painting and didn't say anything.

There was a TV hanging onto the wall just above the dresser. And a door to the walk-in closet. She walked into the walk-in closet and saw his clothes hanging arranged from the lighter to the darker shade. Who hangs clothes in order of shades? Then she noticed how his towels were also nicely folded and placed in some order. She pulled a drawer and saw his ties placed in the order of colors. The next drawer had his underwear and then socks. She secretly smiled. 'How is this man so organized?' Even the condoms in the washroom were placed in the order of color.

"Wow. You are so organized. Everything is in order. How do you have this much time?" She asked.

"I have a helper. She comes once a week and helps me out." Rahul went close to Sasha, moved her hair from her neck, and kissed her.

"Oh," she moved away again.

Rahul held Sasha really close to him again and kissed her under her ear.

Sasha broke out of his arms, walked out of the closet, and smiled. "No. We are just friends. Remember?"

"Yes, we are. Friends with benefits." Rahul held her again in his arms and locked her tight. He had big biceps. Sasha was not big or muscular. Her hair was down and fell over her shoulders.

Sasha pushed him off again and tried to get out of his arms.

"Yaa right. Is that why we are hanging out? No! I don't go to random strangers' houses. Of those I just met in the café." Sasha fixed her hair.

Rahul took his shirt off. He held Sasha tight in his arms, moved her hair off her face, and kissed her again on her neck.

"Stop. I can't. I am sorry, Rahul," Sasha struggled to push him away this time.

"It's ok, baby girl. The night is young, and we both are intoxicated. Let's have fun." He held her tight in his arms. Sasha was still very intoxicated.

She couldn't use any force to release herself from this man's arms.

Rahul didn't stop. He removed her shirt , ripped her bra, and threw her onto the bed. Sasha was just in her jeans with her breasts bare. Sasha covered her breasts with her arms. Rahul sat on top of Sasha and he had no shirt either. He started to kiss Sasha all over her body. She had no energy to fight back, as she was so drunk.

"Rahul, please stop. I can't." Sasha held his hands as he sat on top of her and tried to kiss Sasha.

"Oh, I know what it is." He got off her and turned the lights off. Sasha sat huddled and covered her breasts with her arms.

"Don't be shy, baby girl. Let's make the best out of this gorgeous night." Rahul held her arms and nibbled on her breasts.

"Rahul, it's not about the light," she slurred as she sat up holding her breasts. Her hair fell on her face. Sasha tried to get out of the bed, but any effort was useless. She was way too drunk to lift herself out of his bed.

Rahul got on top of Sasha again, kissed her neck and held her breasts. Sasha tried to escape this

153

situation she hadn't intended to be in, and used force to push Rahul back with both her hands. Rahul kissed her on her neck and sucked her nipples.

"Rahul, stop. It's rape. I don't allow this," Sasha pushed him away.

"Rape? What the fuck are you talking about, babe? You agreed to this. You came over and have been drinking with me for the past two hours," Rahul still tried to kiss and hold her.

"That doesn't mean I want to have sex with you. I came over because you said we are friends." Sasha got up and picked up her bra, and put it on.

"Yes, friends with benefits, I said. You were supposed to be my booty call," Rahul sat on the bed topless. Sasha could see his chest. But she had come because they were friends.

The irony is when you want someone for only sex, you lose the potential to be their friend. Would you not want that human that you like so much to be your friend forever, rather than just have a few sexual encounters? Sasha actually liked Rahul. He seemed such a nice man, but not right now. He was like a monster who made her drunk so he could take advantage of her.

"Yes. Benefits. I thought you needed my help with something," Sasha said, getting away from the bed.

"Like what? Benefits mean sex. Have you not heard of this term before? Or are you just acting as naïve?" Rahul questioned her, and his voice was stiff.

"I am sorry… There is some misunderstanding. I thought we were going to be just good friends, and that's it," Sasha took her T-shirt and put it on.

"It's just sex, okay? It's not a big deal. All I wanted was to hang out with you and have a good time. But you just fucking ruined it. Please leave." Rahul made no eye contact with Sasha as he told her to leave his place.

"What?" Sasha buttoned up her top. She was in shock at what he was saying.

"Yes, leave. You ruined my perfect evening. I wanted to just have a good time. But your Indian mind I guess, is way too congested."

Sasha had tears in her eyes, but she couldn't afford to shed them. She had to get home somehow. She could not afford to show the world what humiliation feels like. Just because you don't know the exact context of a phrase. Or she was not even focused on having sex?

She grabbed her purse and shot out of the door, still trying to walk straight. All that she had drunk was still in her system. There was a flood of emotions inside her, and a very high urge to cry and vomit! Sasha took the elevator and got out in the lobby. She walked out of the door, found the alley, went behind a dumpster, and puked all that she had drunk and eaten. Then she sat down and cried.

Not for a second had she thought that friends with benefits could mean sex! Even when it was so clear. And she had thought it was a casual visit to her guy friend's house. Sasha had a thousand thoughts going through her mind. How could she miss the benefits part? Or was she just so desperate to make friends in this new world that she dared to show up at a stranger's house all alone? Well! Now he was definitely a stranger and an asshole.

She wiped her eyes carefully so the makeup left wouldn't smudge. She must take some transit home. It was a walk of shame. Shame that she did not consider benefits could be something else, or shame for being so ignorant and naïve! She wiped her face and smelled a strong scent. It was the smell of human urination. She got up and puked some more and tried to walk back onto the road.

In the corner, she noticed a person lying on the ground, watching her walk as he smoked and looked at her. They made eye contact.

"Miss, you have some change?"

"Actually, I don't have some change," Sasha still had some effects of intoxication left.

"Can I buy you some food?" Sasha asked the homeless man.

"Oh, that will be kind of you, miss." The man had winter white hair, and his face was time-worn, but he had a friendly smile.

"What is your name?" Sasha and he were walking on the sidewalk toward the convenience store that was just around the corner. May be ten minutes' walk away.

"George."

There was silence between them as they were walking.

"Miss, I saw you crying. You ok?" The man questioned.

Sasha wanted to cry more and tell him everything that had just happened. But it was so embarrassing that even a homeless man would make fun of her. Who doesn't know what friends with benefits means in today's time? Or was she so mesmerized by Rahul's looks that she didn't even pay attention? Whatever it was, she could not ever tell this to anyone. This truth would go to the grave with her.

"Oh, I am fine. Thank you. You can call me Sasha." Sasha tried to hide her tears. But what better can you do to fix your mood? To sit and talk and help someone at the same time?

"Hello, Sasha," he smiled.

There was a silence between them.

"Let's walk to the pizza store," Sasha broke the silence.

"Yes, sure," the homeless man started to walk with Sasha.

"How did you get here, George? Like you seem to be a fine man?" Sasha questioned him.

"Well, Miss… I used to have a family, but I wouldn't stop gambling. I gambled everything. I started to steal things from my wife. I took a mortgage on my house and that is how I got here. Miss, it's all my fault." The homeless man kept walking with Sasha.

"Oh. Sorry to hear that. Who else is there in the family?" Sasha had lost the effect of alcohol.

"I have two daughters. My wife doesn't let me see them. It's not her fault. When you lose control over your mind and do things, you will eventually pay the price."

Sasha was listening to him. She didn't know if he was lying or not. But why would he lie to her? They were strangers. They would never meet again. For some reason, it was a lot easier to talk to strangers than to someone you know.

It was getting dark. The sun was down. It was 11:00 pm and Sasha was walking with this man alone. They both had nothing to lose. Sasha had nothing and this man also had nothing. It was just the two of them standing alone and this was the bare minimum she could do to make his life a little better.

They reached the door of the pizza store.

"You have some preference?" Not sure why, but Sasha didn't ask this man to come in with her.

"No miss. Whatever you think you can get me. I am hungry." The man also didn't show any urge to walk into the store or ask for anything in particular.

Sasha walked into the store and got him some chips, chicken, and some pop. She walked out of the door with a bag and handed it to the man.

"Thank you miss. I appreciate it." He took the bag and looked into it.

"You know what happened? I thought I had made a friend, but he turned out to be a monster." She looked at the man as he was looking into the bag.

He didn't respond. Maybe he never heard what she said to him.

Sasha walked out on the road and took a cab home.

Chapter – 18

The day at the café was not so busy. Sasha couldn't tell anyone her story of what happened between Rahul and her. Good thing she had never told anyone where she had gone. Life is much easier when people don't know all of it. There are fewer questions and fewer things to be answered. She was quiet. The days were going by. Every day felt like a struggle. How could she be so stupid? Not to know what friends with benefits meant? Or maybe she was not even paying attention. She was trying to make friends. She had no one in this country she could go to. She would eventually need some friends. There was an opportunity to make one, and she had taken it.

Rahul never came around after that. She checked her phone, and there was no text message or a call. Not even to say sorry. There was frustration. She didn't even have a chance to explain. But he could have said sorry, couldn't he? The days were passing by, and work made her forget about Rahul. The lifestyle in this country was fast. She had to make money and pay her bills, and so did Nikki and Ira. But then there were weekends, get-togethers, and the birthdays.

It was THE day. "All right, we are all set to go, girls." Nikki was in her leopard print dress with her five-inch heels; it was her birthday.

Sasha, Nikki, and Ira were all dressed up. The living room had makeup and clothes all over. You play with Barbies and then you become one! Both the girls looked like they had come out of a magazine. Sasha blended in with them in the dress Ira had given her to wear and the matching shoes too.

All three of them were all ready to go to the club. Sasha looked just like them from the outside, but was she so from the inside? She was furious. Sasha wanted to know what happened.

"So, the limo should be here any time. We can go around the city and drink and have some fun," Nikki drank out of the glass.

Ira poured some wine for Sasha and passed it on to her.

"We will have a pre-drink and then we can go and drink some more and party in the club. Cheers," Ira proposed a toast.

Sasha just listened to everything they were saying. She was already over what Rahul had done to her. She must not tell these girls what happened. They would most likely laugh at her. She was also frustrated at herself for not being able to grasp the idea of how a man could think of her like that. She was working at her café and was being nice to a man. There is a world outside and then there is a world inside every human. A mystery like an ocean.

Sasha slowly sipped on the wine. She had to see what would happen, and she couldn't lose herself. She must not get drunk.

"Oh, girl… Drink up. We have to party all night. Sasha, you want to blaze with me?" Nikki took a sip out of her wine glass.

"No. Thank you. But I am very excited about this party. Happy birthday, Nikki," Sasha hugged Nikki. Then they both hugged each other. Nikki turned up the volume of the music. They all rocked to the music. Ira, Nikki, and Sasha all had glasses in their hands. There was no one they had to answer to, and they could come home whenever they wanted.

It was almost 7:00 p.m. Nikki's phone rang.

"Ok, girls, it's time. We shall proceed to the limo and party tonight. I have made reservations in Cabana. The limo guy just called and said he should arrive in a few minutes." Nikki poured some more wine into all three glasses. They all drink. Ira and Sasha carried liquor to have in the limousine.

The bevy of three got out of the door. They stood there and waited for the limousine to arrive. The limo pulled over to the side. There were six more girls in the limo. All Nikki's friends.

She saw them hug each other. They all got into the limo and the driver put the music on. There were lights on the roof and everyone was happy and in the mood to dance. There were cups and drinks. Ira passed Sasha a cup. This was her happy place. She was with her roommates and now her new friends. There were no men. No men to tell her to be friends with benefits. Somewhere in her heart, she was angry at Rahul. She had liked him. Emotions come out more when one is intoxicated. Sasha was a little buzzed, but she must not shed a tear. She had to save this makeup until the end of the night.

"I am loving it, Nikki. Thank you for inviting me and thank you Ira for helping me with a dress." Sasha didn't know anyone besides Ira and Nikki. Emotions run high when you are drinking and Sasha realized these two girls were the only ones she had in this new world.

"Oh, it's ok, Sasha. Let's just have fun tonight," Ira hugged her as she fixed her hair.

The limo had all ethnicities under one roof. Nikki introduced Sasha to all her friends. Sasha smiled and said hello.

Jodi opened a champagne bottle and poured it into everyone's glass. And everyone screamed Happy Birthday, Nikki!

Sasha was blown away by everything. Maybe everything was also amplified by the alcohol in her body, but right now she could see a celebration. Nikki was wearing a happy birthday sash and a little tiara.

There were lights on above, on the ceiling. The music was loud and she could see the road and people on the road. Everyone was dancing and talking. Everything was just so beautiful. Sasha could not be happier than this. She finally was with some people she knew. She was making new friends. The limo drove around and Sasha just quietly watched everyone. Ira was loud. Sasha was still so surprised how this girl from India was this open and knew so much.

After half an hour of driving, the limousine pulled onto the side. The driver was an Indian man dressed in a nice suit. He had a thick golden chain as a necklace and a big golden bracelet on his wrist. His height was probably six feet, and he was very well-built and in his forties. He opened the door. All the dressed-up girls got out of the limo. Sasha was the last one to get out. It felt like this car was a basket full of flowers, and they all were the flowers.

"Hello, ladies. My name is Randy. I am your driver for the night. Please give me a call when you ladies want to go home. I shall come to pick you up," Randy, the limo driver, told everyone.

"Thank you, Randy," Nikki told the man.

There was a line-up at the door, and a tall, well-built man was standing in front of the door. Nikki went up to the guy and hugged him. He was the bouncer and also a friend of Nikki's.

"Oh, she must party a lot? Nikki knows the bouncer?" Sasha smilingly asked Ira, who stood next to her.

"Well, I think they went to school together. She told me when we were planning her birthday. That's why she booked this club," Ira explained.

"All right girls! Let's go in," Nikki said.

They all skipped the line and went into the club.

The music was loud and the lights were dim. Nikki went up to the table and everyone followed her. Sasha just sat there quietly and watched everyone. Soon a gorgeous blonde-haired server arrived in a mini skirt and a white top, carrying the bottle of "Gray Goose". She poured alcohol into everyone's shot glass and left.

All the girls picked up their glasses and downed the shots. Nikki poured more for everyone and before she even knew, everyone hit up the floor. Sasha who was now a little buzzed, rocked to the music. Slowly, the club started to get full. Sasha sat on the couch and watched everyone. This was one of the most beautiful nights she had ever had. She was with people she knew; she was free, and safe! Sasha danced with the girls.

The night went on; before she knew it, it was 1 a.m. Everyone was there, but Ira was missing.

Chapter – 19

Aaron, a forty-five-year-old businessman with a boyish grin, drove a sleek black BMW convertible along the Marine Drive in Vancouver as Ira sat beside him beaming. It was dark outside, and the roof was down, so the wind blew Ira's long black hair, seemingly disappearing into the night sky. She was exhilarated by the drive, but also that she had left the party with this man. As they were leaving the club, for a moment she thought about going back, but Ira liked this man's convertible BMW.

Ira twirled her dark locks between her fingers and smiled at Aaron, "You were looking at me. I knew you were going to hijack me from the party."

Aaron glanced back with a smirk, "I'm not hijacking you. We're just going for a drive."

His eyes lingered on her fit body, which had been tucked into a dress. Ira noticed and motioned for him to keep his eyes on the road. "Where are you taking me, Aaron?"

"Nowhere. Just a drive along the beach, so I can talk to you," he replied, rubbing her legs with his hand.

"Awe, you are so sweet," she smiled.

He held her hand and kissed each of her fingertips. "So, what made you leave with me tonight?"

Ira shrugged innocently, "Why not? You seemed to be a gentleman."

"Right." Aaron smiled as he put his hand between Ira's legs, but she pushed it away.

"What's wrong?" Aaron asked Ira.

"I don't even know you. Didn't we meet just now?" Ira replied.

"What do you want to know?" Aaron, the Caucasian man, asked her.

"What can you tell me? Where do you work?" She looked at him.

"Well, I own a business." He looked at her and moved her hair away from her face.

Aaron pulled out a bottle. "Have some cognac. It's a German blend. I bought it when I was in Germany on vacation."

Ira eyed him, "I am already drunk; that is why you were able to pick me up. Are you trying to get me even more drunk?"

"Don't worry. You are in safe hands," he assured her. "It will keep you warm. It's chill with the roof down."

Ira took a shot. Aaron broke into a mesmerizing smile. Ira giggled and took a few more.

After a few minutes, Ira noticed her confidence had grown. "I like you, Aaron. You are very cute and gentle."

"Oh! Thank you. Those are some kind words. Are we friends now?" Aaron rubbed her bare leg and gave her a smirky smile.

Aaron cruised along, glancing sideways at Ira. He caressed her smooth thigh. Ira took his hand and slipped it between her legs. Feeling her warmth, he slowly puts his finger inside her underwear. Ira didn't say anything; she just spread her legs for him.

Ira was drunk. Ira mused to herself, 'If this is what he wants, if I am what he wants, then what is wrong with that?'

"Ira, do you want to go to my place? I have a house nearby that I'm sure you would love to see."

Ira nodded. Inside, she was bursting with excitement that he was taking her to his house. She would see how he actually lived, but at the same time, she was nervous, because she didn't know who would be at his place. Did he have any family living in the house?

Aaron turned up the music as he bent around a corner up a tree-lined lane. Aaron's eyes drifted down Ira from top to bottom. Soon, the convertible pulled up in front of a driveway. Aaron opened the garage door with a minuscule remote and coasted right in. He got out of the car and opened Ira's door for her. She was not used to this kind of care and attention, but she was loving it—a gentleman who knew how to treat a woman and he was wealthy too. Did she just hit the jackpot?

The moment Aaron opened the door to his home, Ira's mouth dropped open, stunned by how big it was… and quiet. She realized there was no one in the house.

Ira inquired, "How come there's no one here?"

"This is my sanctuary, my place to take a break from the city. I have a housekeeper who comes to clean during the days, but tonight, it's just you and I."

Grabbing her hand, he led her to the bar and poured another drink for her. Ira knew if she had any more alcohol, she might puke, but accepted the glass nonetheless.

Aaron leaned in and kissed Ira. His warm, wet lips sent shivers down her body.

He pulled away, "Come, let me show you around."

Aaron opened the double oak doors to his bedroom. "This is the master bedroom."

Before Ira could say a word, Aaron took her into his arms. Ira let him do what he wanted. He was a powerful, important man and very handsome. Besides, the cognac seemed to have sapped her energy or will to fight back.

Giggling, she pulled away, "I need some fresh air." She sauntered onto the balcony and glanced at the swimming pool, which was all lit up. Aaron came up behind her and slipped Ira's dress off. She didn't stop him. Ira was revealing her full breasts, almost popping out of her pink push-up bra. Aaron came in closer, took one out gently, and nibbled on it.

With lust-filled eyes, Aaron whispered, "You are so beautiful."

"Thanks," Ira caressed her breasts and pinched her dark, well-rounded nipples.

Still in her heels, Ira caught a glimpse of her long, lean, naked body in the reflection of the balcony doors. "I can walk like this in the house?" she asked.

"Why not? This is my house, and no one is here," Aaron held her hand and guided her to a small bar in the corner.

"Who else is in your family?"

Aaron went behind the bar, laughing, "Why do you want to know everything? Relax. Take it easy. What do you want to drink?"

Ira, too drunk to care she was drunk, replied, "You're funny. I will make my own drink."

Ira stumbled behind the bar and pushed Aaron away playfully, "I hope you don't mind a naked bartender?"

Aaron sat on a bar chair and grinned.

Ira reached for a bottle and two glasses. She filled them with ice and rum, leaving just enough room for a splash of juice. She handed one to Aaron and toasted, "To new friends."

"Do you usually go out like this with strangers, Ira?"

"Are you a stranger? I thought we were friends."

"No. I am a stranger."

"Really? Maybe it's the other way around, because I know who you are." Ira laughed, "A businessman, Aaron."

Amused, he replied, "Smart girl."

"So, you never answered my question. Who else is in your family?"

"My two beautiful children and my wife." He sipped on the whiskey that he poured for himself in a crystal glass.

Ira was stunned silent for a moment, not knowing how to react. She didn't think he was a married man. He had no ring on. This really great guy was nothing but a cheating bastard.

All of a sudden Ira was not drunk anymore. Who says you have to sleep it off? A shock will sober you up way quicker. She wanted to puke. Not because she had a belly full of rum and cognac, although that didn't help. Ira realized then, that a successful man will not pick a woman from a bar for a relationship. He will bring her to take her clothes off. Ira wanted to throw up as she was standing nude behind the bar in the bedroom of a rich Caucasian man, and she had no clue how to get out of this mortifying experience.

What was she thinking? That she could have this rich man? As her boyfriend? She laughed in her head. She was young and he was probably twenty years older than her. Isn't that what an older single man wants? A young, pretty girl as a girlfriend? But now she was stuck. He was a married man.

But then she didn't want to feel like an idiot going out with a man who looked a little more mature than her. She liked him; maybe he was not happy in his marriage. She gave it another try.

She asked Aaron a question, "Who do you like more? Me or your wife?"

Aaron frowned, "My wife, of course. I have had many women come into my life before, Ira, but no one can replace her."

Ira said nothing. She placed her glass on the bar and stumbled onto the patio to get dressed.

As she struggled to put on her bra, Aaron grabbed her wrist. He spun her around close to his chest. Holding her around the waist, he looked into her eyes, "What happened? Did I say something wrong? I thought you were with me for the whole night?"

He tried to stop her.

Ira turned her embarrassment into anger, "Step back, okay. I'm leaving."

"Where? And how? We are both too drunk to drive."

"I'll walk." Ira tried to maintain some semblance of dignity as she struggled to put on her tiny denim shorts.

"At least tell me what happened. Did I offend you? I am sorry," Aaron tried to stop her, but Ira finished getting dressed and walked out of the bedroom.

Aaron stopped her at the front door and held her arms, "Why are you doing this? Let's have some fun. Please."

Ira peered into his eyes while she wiggled her arms out of his hands. "You couldn't even fake not loving your wife for one night, and you expect me to fake making love in your bed? Really? I don't need you; you need me. Now, let go of me because nothing will stop me anymore."

"But why? What did I do? You agreed to this," Aaron begged.

"I really thought we could be something, but you just want sex." She looked at him in question.

"So, you would rather be a gold digger and pick an older man? I just wanted to have a good night with you," Aaron looked at her as she stood at the door.

Ira stormed out of the house and Aaron let her.

Chapter – 20

The driver pulled the limousine over, got out, and held the door for Sasha, who was the last one to be dropped. Nikki and Ira had both disappeared from the party.

"Miss, there is one bottle of alcohol left in the limo. Would you like to take it with you?" Randy the driver, asked her as she grabbed her purse.

"Sure. I will take it." Sasha took the bottle. It was now 3:00 a.m. She got off on the sidewalk of her building. She would have to go to the apartment alone. Sasha was still upset about Rahul. She still wanted to tell someone what had happened with Rahul. She was devastated. How could someone be like that? And the alcohol didn't help. Her roommates had disappeared on her, and the effect of the alcohol just made it even worse.

You know, when you are drunk is when your true feelings pop up. Like it takes a mask off people. They act like who they are… happy or sad. It is all there.

Sasha dragged herself to the door and slowly got out as she wiped her drool from her face. She could barely walk and tumbled toward the entrance. The driver held her hand and helped her walk.

She was being walked by a stranger to her building.

"I am sorry," Sasha said.

"It's ok. I am used to it. As long as you get home safe." The driver helped Sasha walk up to the door.

"Have a good night," Randy, the limo driver, dropped Sasha inside the building.

"You too. Thank you," Sasha had no one around her. This limo driver was the only human on this street right now. All you could hear was the fire truck sounds, and the ambulance sounds. The city never slept. It just became more alive and talkative at night! There were sounds of everything. The trees, the gutters, the pedestrian lights, the sound of transit buses, but no humans besides the homeless people who also went quiet after a certain hour.

There was a security man at the reception. He looked at Sasha. Even though Sasha was completely drunk, she felt humiliated walking in at 3:00 a.m into the building. Well, now it was 3:30 a.m.

Sasha was drunk and angry at Rahul. The only thing she could think of was Rahul. Her intoxicated state brought her emotions out. But she had to be nice to the man who was dropping her off. After all, not all men are the same. She couldn't think or walk straight right now. She was tired and her feet were aching from the heels. She went to the couch in the lobby and took her heels off. Then she got up and slowly walked to the elevator trying not to stumble and fall on the floor. She left the bottle on the couch.

Sasha managed to get into the elevator and pressed number 23.

It was Vian's floor. She sat on the elevator floor barefoot, holding her shoes and trying not to fall asleep. Sasha could barely sit straight. Her eyes were closing as the elevator went up. There was intense peace at this moment. No music, no people, just her.

Just then her peace was taken away by the sound of a bell that stopped and the door opened to the floor 23. Without a thought, Sasha walked up to the door and knocked!

180

She leaned on the door and almost fell asleep. Three minutes later the door opened and Sasha fell onto Vian who was topless and in his pajamas.

"Oh. Hi, Sasha. Oh dear, you are drunk." He held her, picked her shoes up, and brought her inside his house. Sasha couldn't even hold on to Vian… he dragged her to the couch and laid her down.

Vian brought a glass of water.

"Sasha. Get up and have some water." He put the glass on the coffee table, sat next to Sasha, held her from the back, and lifted her. He put the glass against her lips as she sipped water from the glass.

Sasha lay back down on the couch. Vian lifted her legs and put them on the couch. He took a pillow and put it under her neck. Then he took a white faux throw that was lying over his brown leather loveseat and put it over Sasha. He then sat there and watched her while Sasha's eyes were closed. He removed the hair that was falling off her face. He gave her a close look again. Her makeup was almost gone. She was in a short dress and her long black hair looked messy. But oh boy! Was she a beautiful girl! Vian couldn't take his eyes off this sleeping beauty. He had many questions. He could sit there and stare at this sleeping beauty for the rest of the night. Vian wanted to kiss her, but not without her consent. She was someone he could fall for. Simple and gorgeous.

After a few minutes, he went into his room and lay on his bed. Sasha was snoring and Vian could clearly hear her snore. It was just twenty minutes since Sasha came in, and Vian was trying to close his eyes. He was still confused. How did this girl end up at his house late in the night? He was staring at the ceiling. He had to go to work in the morning. He took a mask out of his side table and put it on his eyes. His eyes closed for a few minutes, but then Sasha showed up at his door, waking him up again.

"Vian. Can I sit here with you? Please?" She had drool on her face, and her hair was in a mess. She was standing against the wall.

"Oh hey! Sasha. How are you feeling? Yes, for sure. Come sit." Vian took off his black silk eye mask, got up, and made room for Sasha to sit.

"Thank you," Sasha took the corner of the bed but still couldn't sit straight.

"Can I also get another drink of some sort?"

"You are already so drunk, sweetheart. You can't even stand." Vian was sitting up.

"I know, but I really need to talk. I can't talk without getting completely drunk. I am sorry. I showed up at your door this late, but I didn't know where to go," Sasha sobbed a little.

Vian was listening. He was still not convinced about getting her more drunk.

"Babe. We can talk in the morning when you are sober. You can sleep in my bed and I can go on the couch." He got out of his bed and stood up.

"No. You don't understand. I really need to vent this." She looked at him.

"OK. Wait here. Let me fix you a drink. But just one," he told her.

Vian took the blanket, put it over her, and walked out of the door.

Sasha was still very much drunk and had no control over her emotions.

She had tears in her eyes. Vian went to his bar, got a glass, and poured a small drink for her. He brought the glass back. Sasha had tears in her eyes. He passed her the drink. Sasha took the glass and drank up the whole thing in one gulp.

"You know, I got kicked out of a guy's house some time back. I thought he was my friend."

"Like right now?" Vian questioned.

"No, silly. Not right now." She looked at him and was drooling a bit. Vian passed Sasha some tissue to wipe her tears and her drool.

"Where are you coming from this late?" Vian questioned again as he stared at the clock. It was 4:00 a.m.

"Well, I was at a party. And both my roommates disappeared on me. I want some water, please," Sasha asked Vian while she was all wrapped up in his blanket.

There was water on his side table, and he passed her the water. Vian was listening and also sitting there looking at this beautiful girl all alone in his house, quite drunk and talking.

"I just got dumped by both my roommates. I don't know where they went and I got dropped home alone. Let's go back to my question first. Like since when did friends with benefits start meaning sex?" Sasha took a sip from the water.

Vian was still quiet.

184

"You know benefit means helping someone or gaining something, and he said I was his booty call. Now what does this booty call mean? And here you are, so nice to me…" She had tears in her eyes.

"Where did you meet this guy?" Vian questioned her.

"I was working in the café. He came in as a customer. I seriously thought he wanted to be friends with me. What does booty call mean, Vian?" She put her hand on his shoulder and looked into his eyes.

"Sasha! Please get into bed and take some rest. We can talk about this in the morning." Vian helped Sasha lie down in his bed.

"Ok," Sasha didn't question a bit. She had a runny nose. She got in bed, and Vian covered her and tucked her in. He shut the door behind him. He went into the living room and slept on the couch. It was all quiet in the house. All you could hear was the waterfall in his house.

Sasha woke up in the morning. The room was dark, and she had a pounding headache. Oh, it was not her room! She looked around. Wow! She was in this gorgeous bedroom. She got out of the bed and put her feet on the floor. She had cozy slippers to put on as soon as she stepped down. It was a hardwood floor. She was in a lot of confusion. How did she end up here? She got up and opened the door and realized she was in her building, but in Vian's house.

She carefully looked around and found the house was empty. The only sound there was the sound of that gorgeous waterfall in Vian's house. She went into the kitchen and got herself a glass of water. Then she found a note on the white marble counter…

"Call me when you get a chance at 778- 994- 3234. Sorry, I had to leave. I had a meeting. You can close the door and it will lock itself. Have a nice day, buttercup."

Sasha drank some water and read the note. How can you fuck up so much in one night? She could vaguely remember her night. She remembered she went to a party but she didn't know where her roommates went. She walked around Vian's place, went back into his bedroom, and made his bed.

Her head was pounding. She was feeling like she would throw up any second. She definitely didn't want to throw up in this beautiful place. This was spotless… Like wow, she had never seen a house like this before. This was like a hotel.

"All right, Mr. Budha. I have to go now," she talked to the statue in the living room. Sasha gathered herself and walked out of Vian's house and the door closed behind her. She looked back and there was a keypad on the door. The door clicked automatically.

Sasha got in the elevator and punched the number of her floor. Her makeup was all gone and her hair was messy. She hoped no one would get into the elevator. But nothing really mattered. It was not like she was some celebrity. She was just a waitress in a café.

Chapter – 21

The elevator stopped on her floor. She had just left paradise. She wished she could live in Vian's house. It was so peaceful. She didn't mind being his housemaid. But she had just slept in his cozy bed. Sasha was thinking about him. There was one man who wanted to take advantage of her, and then here was another who gave his bed away so she could get some rest. There was one man who made her drunk so he could take advantage of her, and then here was another man who helped her get sober and didn't even touch her. She was wowed by this man.

Sasha still had the note from Vian. She wanted to call him, but she also had a headache. Sasha unlocked her apartment and got in. There was no one. She had no clue where both her roommates were.

She went into her room and got herself some headache medications. Then she gathered some energy and called Vian.

"Hello. You woke up, sunshine?"

"Oh yes. Sorry about last night. I should not have done that. I am embarrassed." Sasha was sitting on her bed.

"Oh, don't be. It's all good. I am glad you trust me. How are you feeling?"

"Thank you, Vian. You are kind. I woke up with a bad headache, and I feel like throwing up."

"Oh, of course. You drank a lot last night. Must have been a good party."

"Yes, it was a good party."

"Well, have another beer to cure the hangover," he laughed.

"Oh no. Not drinking again for a long time. I feel awful," she laughed with him over the phone.

"Well! I won't hold you for too long, but you think you could come to my office and see me when you get a chance?"

"Well, I can, but is there something special?"

"You will find out when you get here. Go to reception and ask for me."

"Ok. I can come in a couple of hours?"

"Sure. I will be here all day. See you soon."

"See you."

They both hung up their phones.

Sasha still had a bad headache. She had no clue why Vian wanted to see her in his office. Maybe he wanted to show her where he worked. That was cool. He was a good-hearted man. He didn't try to take advantage of her when she was drunk and alone in his penthouse.

She hadn't had a very good sleep, but she also wanted to visit Vian. The curiosity in her didn't allow her to sleep. Sasha was still in her dress from last night. She went into the washroom and looked in the mirror.

'Oh no.' She was shocked. Her fake eyelashes were off, and her eyeliner was all smudged up. Her lipstick was off.

'Oh, God! Vian saw me like this?' She again talked to herself in the mirror and wanted to cry.

It was not that she could have him as her boyfriend, but being seen like this by any man on the planet? It was just awful. She took the dress off and hopped in the shower. She was tired from last night, she had a hangover, and now Vian had asked her to visit him in his office. He was the EXECUTIVE PRODUCER/DIRECTOR, but also her neighbor and now a good friend. Sasha had a lot of thoughts processing in her mind. The shower is the best place to think out everything. Even if you want to cry, no one will notice it. It's just you. Sasha got out of the shower and got ready. She got dressed in jeans and a shirt that her mom had given her in India. She put sandals on and walked out of the door.

She looked up Vian's business card and checked the address.

"Oh, right in front of our building? Wow, he can roll out of bed and go to work. What luxury," Sasha babbled to herself.

She went up to the pedestrian light and pushed the button, and after it turned green, she crossed the road. She looked up and saw that it was a tall building. How would she find Vian in this whole building? There were probably a lot of people. But then he had said to go to the reception. The card said EXECUTIVE PRODUCER/DIRECTOR. He must be easy to find.

Sasha entered the building. She was just wowed by the interior. There was a reception desk in the middle, and she noticed a beautiful blonde was on the phone. Sasha approached her and waited for the lady to finish her call.

This blonde was dressed in a mini skirt and a beautiful top. Her body was toned, and her nails were done. She was wearing red heels and was a tall gorgeous lady. Her hair was blonde colored and nicely done and left down. She had blue eyes. Sasha was nowhere like her. She was also not dressed for this office, but she was here to see her friend, who happened to be an EXECUTIVE PRODUCER/ DIRECTOR of this company.

The lady hung up the phone. "Hello. How can I help you?"

"Oh, hello. I am here to see Vian," Sasha's voice shook slightly and she was hesitant.

"Do you have an appointment?"

"No."

"Sorry ma'am, you need an appointment to see Mr. Vian," the lady clarified as she looked at Sasha from head to toe.

That made Sasha more conscious.

"Well, he asked me to see him. Can you please let him know I am here? My name is Sasha."

"Mr. Vian asked you to visit him?" She questioned in doubt.

"Yes."

"Ok. Let me check."

The lady dialed a number, "Hello Vian, there is a lady here at the reception. Sasha wants to see you."

"Tell her to wait in the lobby."

"Ok." The lady hung up the phone.

"Hi. Vian asked you to wait in the lobby. He is in a meeting. Please help yourself with coffee or tea if you like."

Sasha went and sat on the brown-colored leather couch.

Five minutes later, Vian walked out of the elevator and approached Sasha.

"Oh, that was fast. I was thinking you would come around noon. Since you had a very adventurous night…" He hugged her and greeted her.

Sasha looked at the receptionist sitting behind the desk and staring at both of them.

This was her "pretty woman" moment. Sasha's eyes were shining bright, and she was smiling. Vian guided Sasha to the elevator, and they both went up to his office. Sasha, who was still trying to digest that she was friends with an EXECUTIVE PRODUCER/DIRECTOR of a company, broke the silence and picked up the courage to say something.

"This is so cool. You live right across from your home," she said.

There was a little bit of guilt and embarrassment. She had been drunk. What must he be thinking of her? Sasha already had a hangover and very little sleep last night, and this situation she was in was not helping her. Sasha just wanted to go over to the washroom and puke. Puke the hangover and the embarrassment. The worst part was she had no clue what she had told Vian when she was drunk. All she remembered was she had woken up in his bed and found a note on the kitchen table.

Vian smiled and nodded, "Yes, it is pretty sweet, but I have to be close. It saves me a lot of time." The elevator stopped and he showed Sasha the way to his office.

It was a glass-walled office. Everything was so transparent. She could see his entire office from outside. The interior of the office was modern. His desk was amazingly clean with just one laptop on it and a few pens. You would assume there would be lots of files on an EXECUTIVE PRODUCER/ DIRECTOR's table, but that was not the case. There was a yellow-colored couch in the corner and also a mini gym machine for weights and a treadmill facing the window. Then she also noticed Vian had a mini bar in the corner next to the couches. There were two leather brown couches and a yellow couch, which together just made the whole space pop. The coffee table in the middle was like a tree placed in the middle. In the other corner, there was a bookshelf nicely arranged in the order of colors. Sasha was looking at every little thing. She was getting goosebumps. She just was blown away by how humble this man was to take her bullshit.

"Have a seat," Vian asked Sasha who was still in shock with the whole thing. Life has its way, and if there is a night, there is a day. Vian seemed like a light through the darkness. Sasha still didn't know why Vian had called her to his office.

"Very nice and comfy couches, Vian," she complimented, taking a seat, putting her purse on the floor, and trying to keep her eyes open.

Vian got Sasha water from a water dispenser.

"Thank you, Vian. You have a gym at work, a nice living room, a mini library, and a video game station. Wow. So, you own this whole building? You are very rich."

Vian laughed. "No, I don't own this building. We have leased it for five years. No one owns a building. Leasing is what everyone does. Can I get you a coffee or something?"

"No, thank you. I am good. I am still trying to digest the fact that you are so wealthy and I know someone like you. It's pretty amazing," Sasha took a sip out of the glass.

Vian smiled…

"So why did you call me here? Is there something I screwed up last night at your place?" Sasha asked. She smiled. What possibly could have happened, for him to call her so urgently?

Vian laughed, "I love how honest you are, Sasha. And no, you did not screw up anything." He took his glasses off, and that made him look even more handsome. Seriously, a nerd with a very muscular body.

"Well, that's a good start," Sasha smiled.

"You know, I was wondering. I have a vacancy in my office. I thought maybe you should give it a try. Also, you won't have to deal with shitty customers at the café."

"Oh, that's a great idea, but I have no experience working in an office," Sasha said.

"That's ok. You will learn. Nothing is difficult if you put your mind to it." Vian looked into Sasha's eyes as he waited for her answer.

"Ok. I can try. So, when do I start?" Sasha got off the couch. She was in his bed last night and now she was going to work for him. Sasha had goosebumps. She had no clue what life was doing to her.

"Tomorrow?" Vian asked.

"Yes, sir. I can also roll outa bed like you do and show up," she laughed.

There was laughter in the office. Sasha was happy and Vian just looked at her laugh…

"You know, Sasha, you are funny and very honest. I will be happy to have you added to our staff. You had a rough night. Maybe you should go sleep for a bit and come back tomorrow with a fresh mind." Vian got up from his chair. Sasha and Vian walked out of his office door. Sasha was in shock. It was hard for her to even imagine being able to work at such a cool place. Sasha got out of the building. She had a shine on her face and a dream in her eyes.

Chapter – 22

You know there is an outside world and there is also an inside world and then there is a world where it's just you and yourself? Right now, it was just Sasha and herself. She was still very confused and happy at the same time as she walked down the road.

Sasha was imagining Vian's cabin. The interiors of his office were stunning. Not just some plain white or gray colored walls. But inspiration quotes everywhere. Sasha was thinking what had just happened?

How does this man have it all? How is it possible to be so perfect? To be handsome, rich, and successful all at the same time? There were no red flags about this man. Well! Being ridiculously rich and handsome seemed like a red flag of its own. How do you miss red flags? She was slowly figuring out that part. Rahul was a good lesson. To understand a relationship well, you have to be in a relationship.

She was still confused about Vian hiring her to work for him. Why? He barely knew her. Why would he hire her? She had no work experience and she didn't know what she would be doing around his office. The trail of thoughts was racing through her mind. She tried to connect the dots. How did this miracle happen? She was drunk last night from a party, and she was dropped off outside the building they both lived in and then all she remembered was waking up in his bed.

"Oh no. We had sex probably," she slapped her forehead.

"But then I woke up with all clothes on? No… No. Can't be that." She shook her head and realized she was on the road. She smiled.

She tried to think of the conversation they might have had. She didn't seem to remember a thing. She had no idea what she had told him. Sasha was walking down the road, still trying to consume all that had just happened. She could see herself in the mirror of a store and she smiled. 'Wow, I am so lucky.' She wanted to scream at the top of her lungs, but she was still walking on the road. Everything was just unbelievable.

She looked in the mirror outside a store and tossed her hair around.

Life was just getting better. She had just traveled in a limousine, then she had slept at the house of this rich man who didn't touch her and had just given her a job. What else did anyone want from life?

Sasha still had a hangover. It felt like she would puke at any time. You know when you get overtired? You can't either sleep or eat anything? What she wanted right now was some hot water and lemon in it. She also had to call the café. But you can't just quit. She would have to give three weeks' notice. There were rules and she had to follow them. There was the outer world and it was different from what she had…

And then there was an inner world that was trying to digest and adapt to all this together. It felt like a dream and she loved every bit of it.

Chapter – 23

The day was sunny and the afternoon sun was crisp. The sun shining in this city was a festival of its own kind. People in Vancouver named it Raincouver because it was always raining. So, when the sun shone, they dropped everything and got out. The streets got busy and there were people everywhere on the bikes at the beaches.

The sound of chirping birds was replaced by the sound of cars and street buskers. But Sasha was so tired that she could take a nap on the sidewalk. Vian's bed was super comfy. She wished she could crawl back into his bed right now. The bed so soft that it took you right in.

"Aahhhh… I miss that bed," Sasha was somehow keeping herself awake. She got some food from a store two blocks away and walked back to her building.

There was sleep in her eyes, but excitement in her mind. She took the elevator and got into her apartment. She stepped on a yellow-colored parcel with a handwritten message. It was probably slipped under the door by someone. There was no postal stamp on the envelope. There was Ira's name on it. Sasha took the parcel and put it on the table. The parcel was not sealed. Sasha was just happy and excited to get a new job. She was thinking of calling her café and telling Sukh she was no longer working for him. She would miss Patrick and Mike, but well...

The parcel was sitting on the table and Sasha was tempted to open it. But it didn't belong to her. She hesitated but opened it anyway.

When Sasha opened it, she found that there was money in it. She also found a note that was for Ira. So many 100$ bills? Sasha was in complete shock. Who leaves money like that on the floor below the door? She was also confused. But then she dared to read the message....

The note said, "THANK YOU FOR THE BEAUTIFUL NIGHT. YOU ARE ONE PRETTY LADY. LOVE TO HAVE YOU AGAIN."

Sasha was more than confused. She had no clue what was going on. She closed the envelope, licked it, and sealed it. And now she wished she had never opened it. She had many questions. She left the envelope on the table and dialed the café's number.

"HELLO – Galria café. How can I help you?"

"Oh, hello Patrick. It's me, Sasha."

"Oh, hello sweety. What is going on?"

"I am very sick, Patrick. I can't come to work. Can you tell Sukh?"

"Ok. I will let Sukh know."

"Thank you. Also, I am picking up my meds later. Let's meet up once you are off!"

"But you are sick?"

"I am drunk sick. If that makes sense? Let's meet up."

Patrick laughed. "All right, senorita... See you at 5 pm."

Sasha hung up, went to her bed, and promptly passed out!

The day was crazy... But she couldn't wait to tell Patrick she had found another job!

Sasha set up an alarm for 5 p.m. She had only a few hours to rest, but she was excited to share the news with her friend. Before she even knew it, her alarm was ringing. She wished she had a few more hours to sleep, but life was happening. She needed to forget sleep and get on with life.

How do you react to something so unexpected? She would be working with someone so skilled, successful, and good-looking! She must be dreaming. In an office where everyone pretty much looked like walking models on the corridors of an office ramp.

Her hangover from last night was still hovering over her. Sasha gathered herself and fixed her hair, looked at herself in the mirror, and went out of the door.

There were cherry blossoms on the trees. The street view was spectacular. The white and pink colored flowers were hanging from the branches just so they could bloom and fall. Sasha saw some on the roadside. It looked like a gray blanket with flower prints from far away and was quite similar to the night Jasmine flowers she saw in India lying on the green grass. She was distracted by the flowers and forgot she was tired. Thoughts were racing through her mind.

Sasha walked to her café, or rather, her former workplace soon-to-be. She waited outside for

Patrick to get off. This was not something she had ever dreamed of. The only part scary about this was that she had been drunk in Vian's apartment. And the same man was going to be her new boss. How could a terrible mistake land her such a great job? Well… she was drunk! So, it could be blamed on the alcohol, but now she couldn't afford to lose this job. She would have to quit the café…

It was almost closing time. Patrick came out and walked toward Sasha.

She smiled.

"Oh, now I am curious," he said.

Sasha dragged him by his arm and they both walked to the nearest pub.

The pub was loud. Sasha and Patrick had walked into a busy pub. It was almost 6:30 p.m. There were high wooden stools along the bar and there were booths in red-colored leather. The large yellow lights hanging from the roof and casting light onto the booths made them look even more vibrant. They took seats at the bar on the stools. People were drinking and eating food. Sasha noticed some very beautiful blonde servers walking around with food and some with empty dishes. The music was mixed. Sasha felt alive again. She was tired, but this atmosphere was just something to make anyone feel alive. The air conditioning inside the pub made the environment more pleasant. Even though it was not hot outside, the coolness inside the pub felt amazing.

"I will skip the drink," Sasha said as she climbed up onto the stool.

"Why? Let's have a beer," Patrick insisted.

"I can't. I still have a hangover from the girls' night out," she made a face with her lips and raised her eyebrows.

"Oh, party girl… beer is the cure. You have another drink to feel better."

"What are you saying, Patrick? Have more alcohol to fix the hangover?"

"Yes, doll. Trust me," Patrick smiled.

The bartender came up to them and asked what drink they would prefer.

"OK if you say so," Sasha looked at Patrick and then at the bartender.

"Yes. What can I get for you?" The bartender who was a Caucasian man and very well-built asked Sasha. He had blue eyes and dimples on his cheeks.

"I will take a beer please," Sasha smiled.

"And can I please get a pink martini," Patrick smiled at the bartender.

"I will be right back with you guys' drinks. Anything on the menu you would like to order for food?" He asked.

"We are good with the drinks so far," Sasha told him and Patrick agreed. The bartender took the menu and walked away.

"You were flirting with the bartender?" Sasha asked Patrick with a smile.

"Why not, Babe? He is hot shit," Patrick pretends to drool and Sasha laughed at him.

"So? Are you going to tell me all about your girls' night out? Is that why we are here?" Patrick asked Sasha.

"No. I have something else to tell you." The drinks were there. Sasha sipped on her drink and looked at Patrick.

"Something else? Shoot, darling. I am very curious." Patrick sipped on his pink martini. He was wearing a dog collar on his neck and his nails were painted. Sasha loved how free this man was and he was always happy.

"I am starting a new job tomorrow," Sasha raised her eyebrows as she took another sip of her beer.

"What? That's not what I was expecting. I thought you would tell me all the dirty stories from the party. Where and how did this happen?" Patrick looked at her in shock.

"Well, everything happened really quickly. I don't know, but in just one night I went for a limo party and a girls' night out... slept at my new boss's house, and got a new job in the morning. I am trying to add up, but I need to quit."

"Wow! Slow down for a second, girl. Let me add all this up. You slept at your new boss's house? That does not sound right." He drank some more from his glass.

"It's not like what you are thinking. I was drunk and passed out in his bed. He is my neighbor. I don't know how or why, but I did go to his floor when I was drunk."

"Then what is it? It all sounds so wrong, Sasha," Patrick looked at her with suspicion.

"Ok. Well, my new boss happens to live in the same building as me, but then after the party, I was too drunk and went to his penthouse and passed out there. I found a note for me in the morning that said 'See me at my work'. And when I went there, he offered me a job," Sasha finished her drink.

"Wow… you are lucky. I am so happy for you. You know what you will be doing?" Patrick gave Sasha a tight hug.

"Well. I don't know yet," she made a face and raised her shoulder. Patrick was still quiet as if he was trying to figure out. He was listening to Sasha.

"I asked him if I could be his housekeeper. He lives in a penthouse and has a patio, and I think a rooftop patio too." She had this shine in her eyes like she had found some treasure.

Patrick laughed… "You asked him if you could be his housemaid? Is he hot? How old is this man we are talking about?"

"Oh my God, he is so cute. He is an EXECUTIVE PRODUCER/DIRECTOR. Like in the late thirties,

I would say." Sasha asked for water and the bartender passed her a glass of water with ice. She sipped it and there was a brief silence.

"Mm… oh my! Girl, I think he likes you. Like what girl passes out in some EXECUTIVE PRODUCER/ DIRECTOR's house? I mean penthouse with a patio, and the next day he offers you a job? Whatever it is honey, this needs to be celebrated." Patrick waved at the bartender.

"Can you please get us two tequila shots?" Patrick asked the bartender with a smile as he tilted his head.

"Patrick. I can't have anymore. I will puke and puke at you," she told him.

"This is a celebration drink. Don't say no. And once you marry this rich man? Don't forget about me," Patrick laughed hard.

"Thank you, Patrick, there is nothing like that between us. Just a person in need of a job and he happens to be an EXECUTIVE PRODUCER/ DIRECTOR," Sasha slammed down the tequila shot, licked her hand, and put a lemon in her mouth.

"Ok. Ok… let's take this shot to your new job," Patrick also took the shot.

Sasha licked her hand again and took another shot.

The night was young. She really wished she could stay, but she also had a new job to start and this was probably her farewell drink with Patrick.

"So, looks like it is our last meet? Since you are quitting?" Patrick opened his arms and Sasha hugged him.

"Yes, looks like it," Sasha said.

Chapter – 24

She was in the office building. Sasha was dressed in her black pants and a white shirt that she used to wear in the café. The only thing that was missing was the apron. And she had switched her black shoes with black heels. Overall, not too bad. At least in her opinion, her slim body and white tucked-in shirt looked sleek on her with her long, black hair down.

Sasha went up to the reception.

Sasha had no idea what she would be doing in this place. Standing under this tall ceiling with a big chandelier hanging in the middle and people walking in and out of the building, it felt as if she was just a tiny molecule in this big universe. She had no experience, but she was all ready to learn whatever came her way.

"Hello," Sasha walked up to the receptionist's desk. Sasha was nervous. She had no clue what she would be doing. She had not worked in an office before.

"Oh, good morning, Sasha. I am Cathy. My apologies for yesterday. Mr. Vian wants to see you in his office," Cathy smiled and directed her to the elevator.

"Mr. Vian's room is on floor 14 to your very left," Cathy smiled.

Sasha got in the elevator and she pressed 14. The elevator went up and stopped. She got out and walked into the corridor. She noticed film posters from Hollywood on the walls. 'Wow this is amazing,' she thought, fixing her bag on her shoulders. As she approached the office, she was even more nervous. Her mouth was dry and she had sweat under her arms. She could feel the sweat dripping from her shirt. There was air conditioning in the building, but she was sweating like she had just run five kilometers.

Sasha stopped at the door which had a nameplate that said 'Executive Producer/Director'. She knocked on the door.

Vian opened the door.

"Oh hey. You made it." Vian took her inside the office.

Sasha had been here before. She was still trying to digest everything. It felt like a dream. Nothing was real. It was like she was the same, but everything around her was changing rapidly.

"Take a chair," Vian was still standing.

"Thank you," Sasha sat down.

"How are you feeling today?" Vian took a seat too. "You were pretty beat up yesterday."

Sasha smiled, "I am better. I slept well. Thank you for asking."

"So, I have staff for everything. But you mentioned to me that you could be my housekeeper?" Vian looked at her.

"Oh yes. I wouldn't mind. I can most likely make a really good housekeeper. I can cook and clean and do all the housework," Sasha tendentiously told him.

Vian put one hand on his face, leaned his chin onto his hand, and listened to what Sasha was saying. He smiled as she was talking. Like he was mesmerized by this woman.

"Well, Sasha," he interrupted her. "I already have one person who takes care of my house. But then,

I have something that needs some attention and I have been putting it off for a while." He paused.

Sasha was all ears as she listened patiently. She nodded her head in agreement. She didn't say a word.

"So, Sasha? I was wondering if you could take care of my personal phone calls and my affairs. Which I can't give to just anyone, but you seem to be the right fit for it." Vian got up and walked away from his desk. Sasha turned her head and saw him watching her.

Vian got a coffee from his espresso machine and passed it on to Sasha.

Sasha had no say. She was still listening. She took the coffee mug.

Sasha paused a minute and then spoke, "OK. That sounds like something I can take care of. Can you please explain a little more what you are referring to?" Sasha took a sip from the coffee and asked him a question. She was comfortable.

"So, basically, manage calls from mom, dad, any other friend and relative, my doctor, or any other related calls. For instance. My mom's birthday is coming up next week… send her some nice present. There might be some travel included. And you would have to possibly take care of all my personal affairs. Book my flights, and might also have to travel with me as well. If that works for you?" Vian took a seat on his chair.

"Ok. Yes. I can certainly do that. So, I am your personal assistant?"

"Yes, gorgeous, you got the assignment well," Vian smiled.

"Thank you. I will need all the personal information for this task."

"Of course. Here it is. A diary that has all the names and addresses. You will need to add these to your database. Here is your laptop… go ahead and set it up."

Sasha took the brand new MacBook. She still was not able to believe she had just hit the jackpot.

"Your desk is in my office for today, and tomorrow we will have your cabin ready. We can share the space for one day. If you don't mind?"

Sasha looked at this man who was well-built and handsome. He was dressed in a nice white cotton shirt and blue pants with an "H" belt on. Sasha notices the "H" on the belt.

She opened her laptop and out of curiosity searched for H belt.

A Google Search gave the Hermes belt's price as 1139$. She let out a sigh and looked at Vian who was already working on his laptop.

She opened the MacBook and turned it on. She had a lot of work to do and a lot of organizing. Sasha opened the diary Vian had given her. There were a lot of entries. She looked through the entries. The diary was full of contacts and notes.

From the corner of her eye, she could see Vian sitting on his chair with his glasses on. His top button was open and she could notice his well-built chest beneath the shirt. How could she not have a crush on this handsome man sitting in front of her? Sasha looked at him once again. She got back to her work. He was out of her league, and also, she must not do anything to risk this job.

Chapter – 25

Vian was on the phone and he was working on and off at his desk. Sasha couldn't focus while this handsome beast was in the same space as her. Sasha had lots to figure out. The first one was the MacBook that she had never used in her life.

You can own a car, but you will also need to know how to drive it. Sasha just didn't own a MacBook and that needed some figuring out, as well as this job she had just landed in.

She was looking at the amazing interiors of his office, then at him, and then at the computer. This had to be a dream. Sometimes when you are expecting the worst, the best shows up. This was what had happened to her, and right at this moment she was in this amazing dream and she hoped it never got over. Almost too good to be true!

Sasha had a lot to learn and she had many questions. She had no friends here. Not like Patrick who always backed her up. She smiled and walked out of Vian's cabin to the washroom. She dialed Patrick and he answered.

"What's up, babe? Talk fast, I am at work," Patrick answered.

"Hey, so I have to work on a MacBook and I don't know how to use it."

"Oh, it's easy. Everything is like all other computers. Just tap on the pad. And if you have more questions, use Google. It has all the answers."

"Thank you, lifesaver," she jumped in the washroom.

"OK. OK."

"So, I can always call you when in trouble?" Sasha smiled as she whispered on her phone.

Patrick laughed. "Yes. You can count on me."

Sasha returned to her desk that was in Vian's cabin. She figured out how to use this new computer. The work took a little longer, but she knew she could do this. Sasha did not lift her head as she dug into work. She had a job to take care of.

The day was half done. During this whole time, Sasha and Vian didn't have any interaction.

Vian shut down his laptop and got off his chair. He walked up to Sasha's desk.

"Let's go grab lunch."

"OK," Sasha had no say. He was her boss. They both walked out of the office. She also liked this man's company. He might be just a boss and a neighbor. But he was too hot not to have a crush on.

They took the elevator down.

"Cathy… Do me a favor. Please cancel the rest of my meetings for the day," Vian said, going up to the reception.

"Ok, Vian. I will have them canceled."

Sasha was quiet as she observed everything. It was her first day. She was just grateful she had this job. The more she saw Vian talking to people, the more she was intimidated and attracted at the same time. How can you be intimidated by someone and be attracted to them at the same time? Well, Sasha was on this boat with Vian. She was sailing…

They both headed toward the door.

"So, Sasha, where would you like to have lunch? I needed to discuss a few things."

"Anywhere you would prefer. I don't have a choice. Also, I am not familiar with the city yet."

"Ok. Well, let's go and get my car and go somewhere?" Vian held open the door for her.

Sasha was still trying to make some sense of and digest what was happening to her. Why was all this happening? It felt like a movie. They both lived just across from their workplace. Like you could roll out of your bed and go to work. But she had rent to pay and he owned a penthouse.

The two of them crossed the road and went into their building's parking lot. This was also where they had first met. Sasha saw the garbage can that was located in one corner of the parking lot.

And now they were at the same spot where Sasha had first met him. By the garbage can!

They both looked at each other and smiled.

But they did not exchange any words.

Sasha and Vian went to where Vian had parked his car, got into his red Jeep Wrangler, and drove out of the building.

The music was on and they were quiet.

"Do you do this a lot?"

"What?"

"You know, hiring some random girl for personal work?" She looked at him as her hair was flowing in the air coming from the windows. Vian drove to Granville Island. He was listening.

"Well, no. But you are not a random girl. You are someone who lives in the same building as mine and are also not my coworker." Vian parked outside a restaurant and they both walked inside.

Sasha smiled again. "Oh yes. You are also my neighbor and right now I can talk to you like you are my neighbor?" She smilingly asked.

"Yes, you can," he looked at her and smiled back.

They were at a restaurant on the waterfront with a view.

They walked up to a table with a menu. Sasha looked at the view. There were boats and yachts parked along the shore. Sasha was keeping it casual even though her stomach was rumbling. She had no idea why Vian had canceled all the appointments.

Maybe he changed his mind? She switched her negative thoughts to positive ones.

"I will leave you with a menu," the server walked away.

Sasha took the menu and looked at it.

"This menu is so complicated," she looked at Vian for help.

"Can I order something for you, buttercup?" Vian asked her.

She smiled and gave another stare at the menu.

"Oh! I will have fish and chips. They look familiar," Sasha closed her menu as she looked at Vian.

Vian smiled and looked at her from the corner of an eye. Sasha couldn't understand his smile. It was a very smirky smile.

The server came up. "I hope you two are ready to order?" He asked as he took out his notepad.

"We will take escargot, Coconut butterfly prawns, and chicken wings for the starters," Vian passed his menu to the server.

"I can also take the lunch order if you guys are ready?" Asked the server who was wearing the name tag, John.

"Sasha, you are ready, I guess?" Vian asked Sasha to place her order.

"I will take fish and chips."

"That's a great choice. And what is it for you, sir?"

"Can I please get a Rack of lamb? And a bottle of wine of your recommendation," Vian looked into the server's eyes as he smiled.

Sasha just looked at this man with temptation. There was a man she wanted to be friends with, but he had some other agenda, and now this one? He was everything any woman would wish for. But why a full bottle of wine? It was afternoon? Sasha was thinking.

"Thank you. I will be right back with your order."

"I want you to try some appetizers."

"Ok. But what is escargot? I have never heard of it before."

"They are snails with garlic butter. Very tasty. I think you will like them."

Sasha nodded with a smile. How can you say no to such a handsome man? Who is also your boss?

"So, what is the purpose of this lunch? You wanted to talk about something?" Sasha took a sip of water. Her mouth was drying up. She was nervous. She had no clue what was coming next. Maybe he was going to tell her that he no longer needed her for the job. Sasha didn't want to jeopardize this job at any cost.

"Well, yes. We need to discuss a few things. You are my personal assistant. So, I want to make you an offer of 1400$ bi-weekly salary. If that works?"

"Oh yes. I like what I am doing… Thank you," Sasha had no complaints.

"Sasha. You have to be very confidential with everything. I will give you one company credit card. Please be very mindful of where and how you use it. Also, please keep track of all the receipts," Vian explained.

"Yes. For sure," she nodded in agreement.

"Also, how about we go shopping after lunch?" Vian casually asked.

"Shopping for?" Sasha was confused.

"We can get you some new outfits for work? Give you a little makeover? It will be fun? No?"

"The food is here." The server poured wine into both their glasses. "Enjoy."

"Thank you, John," Vian smiled.

"You are welcome. I hope you guys enjoy the food. I shall be around if you need me," the server walked away.

Sasha was mesmerized by this man.

"So, Sasha. What do you think? I mean you look amazing, but now you have a new position as my personal assistant." Vian waited for her to answer.

"Well. That is a great idea. But I might not have the funds to get new clothes," Sasha had no choice but to tell the truth.

Vian smiled.

"You like the escargot?"

Sasha took a bite knowing that she was about to eat a snail. The thought of snail made her sick, but she was willing to try anything right now. She was in a dream. She liked how much she was going to get paid. Taking care of this man's personal affairs— how difficult could it be?

She tried the escargot with a sip of wine.

"Oh, actually it is tasty and very creamy," Sasha took another bite.

"Great. I am glad you like it. So, what I was going to say is we can get the shopping done today. And be my guest. I am asking you to shop, so you don't have to pay. Would you like to go shopping?"

Sasha nodded in agreement as she smiled.

He smiled and took a bite and sipped the wine…

The music in the restaurant was loud and the place was getting busy as the time passed by. But these two were in their own little world.

Sasha was talking and Vian was listening to her. He laughed in between. Sasha was talking some mumbo jumbo as she was getting the buzz from the wine. But she didn't care right now. She was happy. This was what she had always wanted…

Chapter – 26

Ira rolled down her window and let the wind touch her face. She was in a BMW SUV at a speed of 120 per km on a highway.

"You are not scared to get in a stranger's car?" Sam, a brown man in his mid-forties was driving his SUV on a highway in the early morning.

She was dressed in a blue miniskirt and a white top. Her hair was down and flowing as the wind from outside the window touched her bare skin and her face. It was still chilly outside even though the sun was out.

"Scared of what? I know you. You are Sam, a brown man I met in a pub. You are married and have a daughter and a son in their twenties. That does not sound scary to me," she looked at him and raised her eyebrow.

It was spring and the days were sunny. They both were driving down the highway in the morning.

Who would doubt their intentions, given that time? Only they knew what they were up to.

"Who do you live with, if you don't mind me asking?" Sam questioned her as he fiddled with music from his steering wheel and tried to put a song on.

"I have two roommates. We share an apartment downtown. I mean, it actually is owned by one girl, but she shares it with us and we give her a very small amount as rent."

The road wasn't busy. It was a quiet Saturday. She had no idea where she was going. If she actually got into trouble, she wouldn't know where she was heading.

"Oh. Your roommate seemed to be very generous?" Sam, the middle-aged man looked at her.

"Well, she is very nice and also a rich dad's daughter. Definitely, we are lucky to be able to live with someone like her."

"And what does the other one do?" Sam questioned her.

"Well, that one? She is pretty naïve, it seems like. She seems to have no clue what is happening in the world." She laughed.

"Why would you say so?" Sam had a curious look on his face. He seemed to be more interested in this girl.

"She doesn't know what brands are. Like who doesn't know what Louis Vuitton is? Or like brand names of clothes. She was in my room once and she had no clue about any of the clothes or purses. It's like she doesn't know a lot…"

"Oh. And what else makes you think she is naïve? What is her name anyways?"

"Sasha. Her name is Sasha. Just about everything. Her dressing style, the way she just talks to everyone. Like she thanked me a thousand times when I lent her my dress for a party and then she sat in my room and asked me so many questions. Like about my nails or eyelashes. It was very innocent." She drank water from her bottle.

"Hmm… must be very new to this world. Does she work?" He asked again.

"Yeah, she is a server in some café…" Ira was venting. She was surprised how someone could be this naïve.

"Do you work?" Sam asked her another question.

"I do. I work a little bit and I am studying to be an architect."

"Smart girl. I didn't know you go to school." He changed the music from his steering wheel.

"Well… I don't tell everyone that. You asked me, so I am just answering your question."

"So, what else do you like to do?"

"Well, not a whole lot. I don't usually have time. What do you do? You drive this big BMW SUV. Must be some business guy?" Ira popped a cooler that had 5% alcohol as she questioned him.

"Well, I am a business guy. And I have a company."

"Company of what?"

"You won't show up at my work or something, right?" Sam questioned Ira as he looked deep into her eyes.

"Why would you say that?" Ira raised her eyebrows.

"Well, it almost happened in the past once. I don't want it to happen again."

"Oh… don't worry. It won't happen with me. I know the rules," she laughed.

"Oh, you do? Well, I am in a construction business and I build houses."

"Nice. No wonder you have so much money." Ira drank out of her can. The road was empty and all she could see was trees on either side and a beautiful mountain covered by white clouds and the sun in a blue sky.

It was like cotton floating in the blue sky with a perfect amount of sun.

Sam looked at Ira, put his hand on her thigh, and rubbed it gently. He moved his hand a little more in. Ira who had the can in her hand, opened her legs a little more. Sam moved her dress a little more and moved his hand closer to her panty. Ira looked at him and smiled. She was a little buzzed after two coolers. She bent down and got another cooler.

Sam pulled his hand out of her legs and put it on the steering wheel.

"Listen, this is a no-strings-attached relationship. I don't want you to think anything else," Sam said as his eyes remained on the road.

"What do you mean?" Ira turned her shoulder to him and questioned in innocence.

"You know what I mean? We meet just for two hours once a week and then you go back to your life and I go back to mine." Sam again made no eye contact with Ira.

There was silence in the car. The only sound there was music. The silence was the agreement between them.

Sam held Ira's hand and rubbed it. The SUV was driving fast and reached outside a cabin. The driveway was of gravel and the tiny house was surrounded by trees. It was painted yellow.

"Oh, this is a beautiful-looking house." Ira ignored what he had just said and changed the conversation.

"Yes. It is a nice place. A small cabin away from the city. My friend owns this place and rents it out like Airbnb." Sam got out of the car, took out the coolers, and went to the front door.

It was 10 am. They both entered the fully furnished cabin. Ira opened the cooler and started to drink.

"So, what were you saying in the car?" Ira sat on the couch as she drank her beverage.

"I meant I love my family and I don't want anything changed. I like the situation I am in," Sam took his drink and went and sat next to Ira.

"Oh. I see. Don't worry. I am not here to fall in love either. We will just have fun." She got up and sat on Sam's lap.

"You have had a few drinks in the car. Hope you are not drunk, babe." Sam pulled her hair back and kissed her on her neck as he held her by the shoulders.

"Yes, I did. But I am not drunk. Just a little buzzed." She took off her mini skirt.

"Oh, baby, you are so beautiful," Sam who had a muscular body and was in his late forties lifted her and helped her sit cross-legged on his lap as she kissed him on his lips.

Sam took her top off and took his shirt off too.

"This cabin is so beautiful. I have never been in one like this. It's so tiny, like a bus," Ira looked into Sam's eyes.

"It is, but not as pretty as you are," Sam held her tight.

"Ahh, that feels good. Hold me tighter please," Ira leaned her head on his shoulder. Sam held her tight and then rubbed her bare back.

"Can I ask you something?" Ira who was drunk held her head as she looked into Sam's eyes.

"Ask away." Sam clutched her breasts and kissed her on her neck. Her long black hair fell onto her back.

"You love your wife?"

"I do."

"Then why this?" She asked.

"Well, it's complicated. Hard to explain. Let's not discuss this." Sam kissed her on her neck as he was talking.

"So, we are friends with benefits?" Ira finished her drink and put the can on the table.

"Yes, we are. And anything you want." Sam unhooked her bra and took it off.

Ira smiled.

"I am trying to buy this LV bag and it won't take my card. Can you please get me that bag?" Ira looked into his eyes.

"Yes, for sure. You can use my card to make a purchase," Sam held her tight and kissed Ira.

"You are so nice, Sam," she put her arms around him.

"Should we go into the bedroom, baby?" he kissed her and asked.

"Yes. Pick me up and take me into the bedroom," Ira held on tight to Sam's neck as he got up from the couch.

She had nothing on but the pink thongs matching her bra.

Sam carried her in his arms and took her to the bedroom. He put her on the bed and took her panties off. He kissed her on her neck. Ira put her arms around him and kissed him back…

Sam dimmed the lights in the room and hopped onto the bed with Ira.

Chapter – 27

Nikki sped through the streets of Vancouver as she smoked out of her pen. The music was loud and it was sunny in North Vancouver in spring. The flowers had all bloomed and for the last two weeks, it felt like there was some life on the planet. All the blooms had died in the winter and their life was renewed in the spring. The time span between the death and the birth was very short. Every tree had flowers and the branches went low. There were petals on some cars. Sasha was in the back seat. She moved into the middle seat so she could see both Nikki and Ira.

Sasha was stunned and happy. She was enjoying this wild ride with her two new friends. She had zero care in the world. And Vian was so generous to get her new clothes. It almost felt like a dream. There was cold and very uncomfortable weather along with this magical time.

Sasha was not complaining right now. She was off for a getaway with her two friends to Whyte Cliff in North Vancouver.

"Ira, did you get your package?" Sasha asked Ira a question. Nikki lowered the volume.

"Yes, I did. Thank you. I was waiting for it," Ira said as she looked out on the road toward the mountains.

"This is very exciting. This mountain is so close to where we live," Ira changed the topic and checked with Nikki.

"Yes. It is. I can't wait to go up the mountain. It's not a very long hike. Just fifteen minutes and then we can just drink our coolers on the top of the mountain," Nikki raced through the traffic changing lanes.

The music went loud again. The drive was scenic. All three of them were happy. The air was crisp and the day was sunny.

"That man you working with… seems very generous," Ira asked Sasha.

"What man? The penthouse guy?" Nikki pulled into a driveway in a park. The parking lot was not very full. Especially since it was a weekend and a sunny day.

"Yes. He is. He just bought me some new clothes for work," Sasha told Nikki.

"Oh, he is the boss. Can I get one please?" Nikki laughed. The girls had drinks open in the car.

Sasha loved the hood drop and this ride. The Beemer was black and had a beautiful exterior.

"You don't need a boss, Nikki. You have great parents who give you everything," Ira's hair was flying in the wind and she tried to hold it in a grip as she took a sip.

"Yes, you are lucky to be born to such cool parents," Sasha nodded in agreement.

"Yeah, I know. My mom is so nice. I was with her last night and we partied together. We both got so baked," Nikki took a cigarette out and lit it.

"Nikki, you know smoking is bad for you? And guys don't like a girl who smokes. I am not trying to tell you what to do. It's your life, but someone so nice should live longer." Sasha was a little buzzed and now she could talk more openly about her feelings.

Alcohol does that to people. You laugh and you cry. It lets you loose.

"You know, sweety? No man has ever tried to take smoke out of a girl's hand, but they will always try to take your clothes off if you are innocent," Ira shared the smoke with Nikki.

"I don't understand what you are referring to, Nikki," Sasha was confused. Her idea of a good girl was a little different. This was not something she expected.

"Well. Babe, this is something you will have to learn on your own. It's not something we can teach you or you can read in a book. All I know is innocent girls are raped, but bad girls are just told they are bad. I'd rather be a bad girl than please the world," Nikki laughed aloud.

"I am still very much confused," Sasha looked at both of them.

"Sweety! You know what they say? Good girls make homes and bad girls make history. That's what I mean… Let's go make some memories for now," Nikki answered Sasha.

"Can't agree any less, Nikki. Men always will try to take good girls' clothes off, but no one will ever dare to take smoke out of a girl's hands. You are in a danger zone when you are this free. Oh, we are here," Ira nodded in agreement. Nikki pulled over her car and parked in a stall. The parking lot was not full. There were very few cars.

Sasha looked at them and was thinking how right they both were. She was feeling the energy of these girls she was sitting with, and for a second, she felt as if she could conquer the world.

Nikki pulled the hood back and they got out of the car. They grabbed their bags and started walking to the beach. It was a beautiful day. The sun was not too hot.

After walking down the hill for a few minutes, they reached the beach. The tide was low and they could see the trail of rocks leading to a big hill.

"So, this is Whyte Cliff?" Sasha asked as she looked over the sea.

"Yes, it is. Isn't it so beautiful?" Nikki took her sunglasses off and put them just over her head.

"See those tiny rocks? We have to walk on them to get to that hill. But let's just set up our little spot. So, we can come back and chill here," Nikki told them.

They had been drinking in the car already and had at least two beers each. Nikki had been smoking, drinking, and driving at the same time. But no one could question that... it was her car. She could do whatever she wanted.

"Wow this is so beautiful," Ira sighed. "I love coming here."

"Yes. Nikki. This is so pretty. I have never seen anything like this," Sasha was stunned.

The girls were in their summer dresses with little jackets over them. Even though it was just the end of April, the days were hot. They opened a beach blanket and put it on the sand. It was a picnic day. They left their food and drinks there and walked onto the rocks.

There was a trail of rocks and they walked onto the rocks and climbed up the mountain. It was a small hike of six to seven minutes and before you even knew, you were at the top of the mountain looking over the sea.

All three of them reached the top. They took their dresses off and got into their bikinis. The girls had their set of drinks and water bottles. The sun was shining bright and the breeze from the sea made their bodies cool.

They found a spot and settled for the day. It was a couple of hours after dawn. Life was good right now.

"This is a celebration of Sasha's new job... cheers, you gorgeous ladies," Nikki raised a toast. They were laughing and talking. The three of them had no care in the world right now. It was just them and the beautiful day.

"I will do your hair and makeup when you go to work on Monday," Nikki offered.

She took a sip out of the beer can. She was stuttering. You know, you always speak the truth when you are drunk. And all three of them had had quite a few drinks on the top of the mountain.

Just when the girls were drinking and laughing, a boat stopped near the mountain. There were boys in it and loud music was on.

"Hey. What is going on?" A boy waved at the three of them.

"Nothing much. What's up with you guys?"

"Just a day on a boat. You ladies care to join us?" The guy asked them.

244

The boys were all Caucasian and there were about four of them as they could see.

"What do you girls think? Should we go?" Nikki asked Sasha and Ira.

"The water is cold to swim out there, Nikki," Ira raised a concern.

"Well. It's not that far. We could hear them from this mountain. Maybe five minutes in the water? We will make some new connections. No?" Nikki insisted.

There was silence.

"Come on. Men with a nice boat. Let's go girls, swim to the boat and party. We still have a lot of the day left." Nikki questioned both Ira and Sasha.

"Nikki, these are strangers. How can we go on that boat? That is a bad idea." Sasha just found it strange how someone could just ask them to party.

"Sweety. This is how you meet people. They don't seem to be bums off the street. They are on a boat," Nikki tried to convince her. Ira had no say. She was drinking and listening to both of them.

"No. But you know. They have a boat. What if they take off with us while we are in the boat?" Sasha questioned again and was still hesitant.

"I don't see a problem. They seem a lot of fun," Ira was drinking.

How can you say no when nothing is in your control? She was with Nikki who could drive her back home. Sasha didn't know how to get back home on her own. You can't fight when you don't know the rules. You just blend in.

"No one will kidnap you, honey. This is Canada and we are going," Nikki told both of them.

All three jumped in the water and swam to the boat that was parked near the mountain they were on. The music was loud and they all got on the boat. The boys on the boat introduced themselves and then the party began. Sasha, Ira, and Nikki were dancing to the music along with all those men, Shawn, Gary, Scott, and Russell. The time was good. They were rocking and dancing to the music. The boat suddenly turned into a party boat. They started slowly sipping on the drinks and talking. Nikki was the loudest among all three.

Scott came close to Sasha. Everyone was a little tipsy. Scott tried to kiss Sasha and she said no.

"Oh, babe, it's ok. I respect your wishes if you don't want to kiss. I just wanted to let you know that you are gorgeous."

Scott was a handsome man in his twenties and he was tall and had a six-pack. He was in his shorts. Sasha was not ready for a man yet. Especially, this white guy. Ira was drinking and laughing with some dude and Nikki was just dancing without a care. The sun was slowly moving toward the horizon, The good time always goes by fast… especially on a boat with friends. The sunset was nearing. The day's end on this side of the world was approaching, and it was time to wake everyone up on the other side of the world, where Sasha and Ira belonged. Sasha saw Ira flirting with all the guys.

How were these two from the same world, but were so different? Everyone has a dark side and what was Sasha's dark side? She kept it secret.

The sun was going down and it was about to get dark. The days were still not long. Not long enough.

"Let's go back before it gets dark."

The girls had fun. They said bye to the guys and then jumped into the ocean and swam to the mountain where they had left their clothes. Nikki picked up her empty cans.

Sasha and Ira picked up their things and walked back down the hill. The water was high. The tide was high and they couldn't see the rocks to walk back.

"Oh no. The tide is high. We are late. The rocks we walked on are now under the water," Nikki said.

"Now what, Nikki?" Sasha asked. Nikki laughed. Nikki never got serious over anything. Everything was funny for her. Sasha couldn't remember if she had ever seen her sober. Nikki was always drinking or smoking something. She was almost always intoxicated.

"Now we swim back, girls."

All three were a little intoxicated. The conversation with the men on the boat had been long. There was flirting going on and the effect of alcohol was less. The swim back to the beach in the cold water made them more alert.

"We have to leave our stuff and swim back, honey," Nikki was laughing.

"But the water is so cold," Ira touched the water.

"It's ok. We will be in the car and we can cozy up in our beds. Also, we don't have much of a choice. We can swim back in the cold and warm up in the car, or die in the cold night on this hill. Not a very hard choice to make." Nikki was still laughing out loud.

All three jumped in the water and swam back. They grabbed their towels and wrapped themselves.

"Oh, my goodness. We didn't die and all the alcohol is also not there in the system. The cold water just made me sober," Ira quickly grabbed her things and they all started walking toward their car.

The girls got in the car and Nikki turned up the heat and the music... The night was still young and the girls were happy!

Chapter – 28

All three were happy driving back to the place they called home. They had each other. Nikki, Ira, and Sasha showered and planned to sleep in the living room and watch a movie. It felt like Sasha had sisters by her side. It felt like family. Even though she was still not sure who these girls were… But they had made it home safe. She was still thinking about how they all went on the strangers' boat and had fun with complete strangers. Would she do it if she was alone? Probably not. She had seen Ira's different side. What was that then? The evening she saw Ira with a man in the living room? The living room where they were naked, was still haunting her. But right now? She saw Ira's leg on top of Sasha's legs, her arm resting on her stomach, and her head leaning onto her shoulder.

How can she be bad? Sasha tried not to think of anything. She had just made some memories that she would keep forever.

There was a dark side to everything. Nikki? She drank and drove. She would kill herself one day if she didn't change. How about Sasha? She thought of herself… She was hiding under a different name. She wasn't Sasha. She was Tara pretending to be someone else.

There was darkness in their lives and they all had something they were running or hiding from. But should you stop loving the person they are? Over the darkness they possess? Sasha distracted herself from her thoughts and tried to focus on the TV. The takeout was there that Nikki had paid for. The pizza and other eats. She would later take the boxes out to the recycling on the ground floor where she had met Vian for the first time. Sasha had some warm thoughts about that meeting. The Bollywood Hindi movie was on.

Sasha smiled and looked at both of them. Ira and Nikki had teased her all day long about her new boss Vian. But she just didn't believe it. How can a handsome and rich man like him fall for her? And even if he does? How could she tell him or would she ever tell him that she was divorced? Oh, the more she was thinking, the more complicated life seemed.

Tired from the day and the unwanted swimming, they all passed out on each other. Sasha with the thought of her new boss. The three snuggled in the living room. The TV was running, but the three of them passed out on the floor like three sisters would.

The night went by fast. The new day was here and it was another day at work for Sasha.

Sasha quietly got up and hopped in the shower. Ira got up and made her breakfast. And Nikki? She lay on the floor with her makeup box and her hair tools. It was her job to turn Sasha into a magical person for her second day at work as a personal assistant.

Sasha got out of the shower and was surprised how her two new friends were awake and were all set to send her away to her new job looking like a doll!

Sasha dressed herself up in the new clothes that Vian had purchased for her. An off-white silk top with a pencil skirt and pencil heels.

"Damn! Girl, you don't look like you," Nikki asked her to sit on the chair and did her hair and makeup.

"Eat a little yogurt before you go, Sasha, for your first day at work. It is good luck," said Ira.

Something Sasha's mother would say to her. Sasha couldn't believe how such a cultured girl could be an escort. It was haunting her. She wanted to ask Ira why. But she couldn't. She tried to tell her heart it was nothing. It was just one time she had seen something, but then there was the package that she had opened up, which contained money. Oh, the whole thing was just awful. But right now, both of them helped her get ready for work. Sasha saw herself in the mirror and smiled.

She was all set to go to work. She was nervous and excited. It was no one but Vian who was her neighbor, and her boss from today!

Sasha got her purse and lunch and walked out of the door. She crossed the road and went to the building across from her apartment. How do you get this lucky? Do you get to work this close to home? Life felt like a dream. Sasha crossed the road and she could hear the sound of her heels while she walked in the middle of the intersection. She could feel the wind on her skin and her hair flowing in the air. It was that moment where you feel you are on cloud nine. She was happy… How did she become thus? She looked at herself in the mirror before leaving. She could not believe she could look so different.

The universe seemed to be rigged in her favor if not anything else.

"Hello, Cathy. Good morning," Sasha went up to the desk and greeted Cathy.

"Oh hello. Good morning, Sasha. How are you this morning?"

Sasha noticed that Cathy had a more welcoming reaction than during her last interaction. Other people were walking on the floor. No one looked at her… Because, this time she just blended in with all of them.

Well, she didn't come the first time to get a job. She was just visiting her new neighbor.

"I am very well, Cathy. Thank you"

"Here is your badge for work," Cathy handed her a new card to access the building.

Chapter – 29

Sasha took the badge and walked toward the elevator. Other people were waiting to get in. Sasha stood between them and waited. The light turned green and the elevator opened. People started getting out. The office looked so busy and then she saw…! Something she never wished she would see again. The last person getting out of the elevator was Robin. Her nightmare!

She hid behind the other people while her ex-boyfriend Robin walked out of the elevator.

Sasha got in the elevator. She was still stunned. She was dreaming while she tightened her fist and cringed. She gathered herself and focused on her first day. It was not about Robin or anyone today. It was about her. No one on the earth could stop her. She didn't want to screw up this opportunity she had just got.

Sasha got out on her floor and went into Vian's office. He was already there. Oh, God! He looked amazing again. His sleeves were pulled up. Sasha's heart was beating fast.

"Oh, good morning, gorgeous. Hope you had a great weekend?" Vian smiled at Sasha. He looked at her from head to toe without her noticing from the corner of his eye. At least he tried, but Sasha was able to see that he had laid his eyes on her. Sasha had forgotten about Robin briefly, but now her mind was racing at more than a thousand miles per hour. Like what? She just saw her ex-boyfriend? Who took off on her without even a word. They had had sex. He was her instructor and her lover. After three months of the love affair, Robin just disappeared. Sasha had every memory run down her mind like a flashback. There was anger, rage, hate, and so much more.

Sasha had a million thoughts going through her mind. And he had lied to her that he was from Australia. Sasha wished she could have stopped him and questioned him or even punched him in the face. Punching his face was probably not enough.

Right now, she had to keep her temper under control. She didn't want to cause a scene at work. Maybe he was just a visitor, she told herself as she opened her laptop. She had emails.

"Mother's birthday; send flowers."

"Send flowers to Karen and a sorry card."

Sasha opened her email with the subject line, "Send flowers to Karen and a sorry card."

Email: from Vian

"Good morning, Sasha,

Please send some flowers to Karen at the address at the end of this email with a note as follows.

'Sorry, Karen, I cannot make it to your wedding. Sending some flowers and a gift.

Cheers,

Vian.'"

Then she opened the other email that was for his mother.

'Send mom a present and some flowers to her address.

Thank you.'

Sasha opened the next email.

'Please book two tickets for LA for next week, Monday. One under your name and one under my name. We have a meeting to attend at the address given. Please make the hotel and all travel reservations. It is a week-long trip, so pack accordingly.'

Sasha got up from her chair and went up to Vian's desk. Vian was busy looking at his computer screen and was on the phone. Sasha went and stood in front of him. Vian gestured to ask her to sit while he was still on the phone.

"Can you hold for a second?" Vian told the person on the phone.

"Yes, Sasha? You have a question?"

"I am going to LA with you?"

"Yes. I need your assistance. Do you have any objection?" Vian looked straight into her eyes.

"No. I just wanted to confirm it. I will book the tickets now and also will send something for Karen."

"Oh. Yes. She is my ex-girlfriend who is getting married. Send her flowers and a gift accordingly."

"Yes. Thank you," Sasha took her notepad and returned to her seat.

Back at her desk, she started booking the tickets. Vian taking her on a trip was nerve-racking and exciting. And seeing Robin again? It was making

258

her angry. With these mixed emotions, she sat at her desk and tried to focus her mind. Maybe it was all an illusion? Maybe she was just in a dream and a nightmare simultaneously.

And Vian had an ex. She was curious to see her. But how did it matter? She was not his girlfriend. He was the boss. There would never be anything between them. She just worked for him and that was the only relevant fact with him.

Chapter – 30

"Mom. Can you send me 500$?" Nikki was driving and on a phone call with her mother. The built-in Bluetooth in the car was on. Nikki searched for something in her glove box while she was driving. She found her smoke out and searched for the lighter. Then she lit her cigarette and rolled down her window.

"Nikki, I just sent you 1000$ a week ago. Where did you use all that money? Did you do cocaine again?" (Voice on phone)

"Mom, I don't do cocaine anymore. I told you." Nikki looked at the passenger seat.

"Then where did you spend all the money?"

"Mom, it was my birthday, right? Don't you think I would party? It is so obvious," Nikki explained to her mother.

"Who spends 1000$ on their birthday? You are so spoiled. Life is not just about parties," Nikki's mother got angry at her over the phone.

"I am the only baby you have, momma. Can you please give me 500? I need to get my car cleaned and get some food in the fridge," Nikki tried to convince her mother again.

"Sweetheart, everyone cleans their car themselves. Why can't you do it yourself?" Her mother questioned her again.

"Mom, I need detailing done. I can't do that. Can I?" Nikki gave her mother another reason.

"Nikki… I am sick of you asking me for money all the time, and then you spend it all partying up. You still have the job, right?" Nikki's mother questioned again.

"Mom. You know if you don't want to give me any money that's fine. I will ask Daddy. Bye."

Nikki was frustrated as she hung up the phone and called her dad.

"Hello," Dad answered her phone call.

"Dad. How are you?"

"Oh, Nikki. I was going to call you. I have signed you up for a rehab. You will be packing your bags and leaving in a month and a half," Dad told Nikki.

"Dad, how can you just sign up for me without asking?" Nikki got frustrated with his statement.

"I don't need to ask you. You are my child and my only child," her dad emphasized.

"But I don't want to go to a rehab," Nikki shed a tear.

"You don't have a whole lot of choice there, sweety. Your mother and I have discussed this. We are sick of you being intoxicated. This is the second time we are trying. For your good health and well-being, this is an important step," Nikki's father had a soft voice and he carefully chose his words.

"But Dad, I hated it the last time. They wake you up early and you have to eat certain foods, and then they make you do activities, and on top of all that no TV or cell phone. I was cut off from all my friends."

"Nikki, you will do as I ask you to. It's all my fault to have spoiled you so much, to begin with. Also, you are my only daughter. Have you thought about what your mom and I will do if you ever have a bad accident with drugs?"

"But Daddy, I don't do drugs anymore," Nikki lied to her father.

"Sweety. You can't lie to me. You are probably high right now too. Do you know the type of drugs that are being sold on the road? They all have fentanyl in them. The overdose death rate is very high in the city. Please take a rehab program. It is only for three months. For your Daddy?" Nikki's dad tried to convince her.

"Ok, Dad. Can I please get 500$ cash for now? I need to get some food."

"Ok, I will put it in your account."

"Thanks, Dad."

Nikki hung up the phone.

Nikki made another call and it was to her workplace.

"Hi. Good morning, Scott. I will be a little late. I am stuck in traffic."

"Good morning. Yes, it's fine. Be safe. See you soon."

"Thank you, Scott."

Nikki hung up the phone and drove over the bridge, cut the traffic, and merged into the traffic toward North Vancouver.

She drove her Beemer to a cul-de-sac and pulled over to the side under the trees. She then picked up her phone and dialed a number.

"Hello."

"Hey. I am here," Nikki told someone.

"Ok. I am just on the street. How much do you want for?"

"Give me now for 140$," Nikki replied.

"Ok. Have the cash ready and I will give you two bags. I have to go somewhere else afterward, so make it quick," said the person on the phone.

Just then a black SUV pulled over and in it was an Indian guy with a turban. Maybe in his early twenties and his name was Am as he told her. It was a Sikh boy wearing a beard, turban, and a black hoody.

"Oh hey. Good to see you again."

The guy pulled over beside Nikki's car and rolled down his windows. Then he handed over a bag with Marijuana and Nikki gives him several loose 20$ bills.

"Hey, Am. What does your name stand for anyways? I am just curious," Nikki took her bags and hid them in the glove box quickly.

"It's Amrit Bath, but never say my name over the phone, please. If I ever get busted, I will have to throw this phone away," Amrit her drug dealer told her. He was tall, about 5'9", and had a sunglass on. Even the day was gloomy and Amrit had his shades on. He had diamond-like studs in his ears.

"What else is new?" Amrit asked.

"Nothing much. But hey, can you drop by my place this coming weekend? I need some coke and some molly," Nikki had her car running.

"OK. Sure. Let me know how much and I will hook you up. I have to go now. See you later," Amit raced his car as he made a U-turn and shot out of the streets.

Before Nikki could even turn around, the car had disappeared in front of her eyes. All she could see was dust flying in the air caused by his tires. She started her car and drove to her work.

Chapter – 31

Sasha was sitting at her desk looking at her emails. She couldn't wrap her head around the fact that she had just seen Robin. If she could, she would have put a bullet through his head. But could she do that?

Probably not. Especially, when she had not even killed a fly in her entire life.

And now she had to send a present to Vian's ex-girlfriend?

And then she was also flying to LA with him? Alone?

Sasha was sitting at her desk confused, scratching her head. She had so much to figure out alone in this new life. She was taking it one day at a time. Was she having fun? Yes, with the girls, Sasha was absolutely happy. She was not able to understand Vian as yet. He seemed so sorted and so complicated at the same time. He had been so warm at his penthouse and taken care of her, but then here at work? He was so cold. They both were in the same room and he had not once looked at her. What if she needed to ask a question? Or he just expected she would figure out everything on her own.

"Ughh," Sasha made a sound.

"Everything is ok, Sasha?" Vian took off his glasses and put them on his desk.

"Yes, everything is ok. I had something stuck in my throat," Sasha looked at her computer as she talked to him.

"This is a temporary space for you. Tomorrow we will have a cabin for you, most likely. You will have your own space where you can work all day without interference," Vian put his glasses on again.

"Ok. Thank you," Sasha smiled.

"Let me know if you have any more questions. I can help you with those," Vian smiled at her.

Gawd, he was so hot with or without glasses. Sasha could walk up to him and kiss his lips. She wished she could, but didn't want to lose her job. The café would not take her back. She had quit without notice. Vian took a sip from his coffee cup.

267

'Oh, that cup is luckier than me that gets to touch his lips,' Sasha whispered to herself.

Her stomach felt like it was an ocean of emotions right now and was rumbling like Hurricane Dorian. It felt like she would throw up. It was her second day and this was the new world. She couldn't screw this up. Sasha had to stick to it and deal with it.

Sasha went on to the airline website.

"Sasha, book two business class tickets and two rooms in a five-star hotel in LA. Sorry, I forgot to give you all the details," Vian put a hand on his phone to block the sound.

She wasn't going to book an economy class for her boss, anyway. Maybe just for herself. Sasha still tried to tell her head she had not seen Robin. Sasha had so much work to do. She was sitting at her desk and doing her research. She would have to deliver a class if she wanted to win this man's heart and that could be done only by how well she handled his personal affairs.

She would have to order some flowers for Vian's mother and get his ex-girlfriend a wedding present. Sasha wanted to know what these women looked like or what their interests were. Sasha went on Vian's

Instagram. She went through his photos and found his ex and his mom. What? His ex was a white blonde girl. Wow!

Life was supposed to be tough and lonely. Tough in the sense she would have to find her way through life. She thought she would have to work in a café for years before she could get some experience and do things independently.

This man completely smote her. His curled long eyelashes and his lips? If she ever got alone with him in the same room? She knew she would just break into his arms like a broken pearl necklace. You know what happens when a pearl necklace breaks? All the pearls scatter on the floor everywhere and they bounce… that was how Sasha felt around Vian. The more she saw him, the more she became obsessed with him.

The name of his ex was Karen. Sounded like an Indian name. Sasha booked two business class tickets for LA from Vancouver and then two hotel rooms.

She grabbed her purse and got off her seat.

"I have to go, Vian, to get the flowers and presents for your mother and your ex's wedding present," Sasha told Vian.

"Why can't you just order it online? Isn't everything online these days?" Vian took a sip of the coffee he had just brewed from the machine in his office.

"I could, but I wanted to see everything in person before I send them out," Sasha replied.

"Ok. Sure."

"I already booked the hotel and the airplane tickets," Sasha was ready to leave the office. More than anything, she needed to clear her head. She needed some fresh air. She needed it to clear her head out.

Sasha took off to the elevator and then out of the office building. She had her heels on. How do you walk in heels? Ughhh! Sasha tried to walk and then got sick of them and took them off. She held them in her hands. Who needs shoes when the streets are so clean and spotless? If she was in India, people might have thought she walked barefoot for religious purposes. Here in Canada, people simply didn't care.

Sasha got into a flower store and looked around. She got pink roses for Vian's mother Irani and white lilies for his ex-girlfriend. Then she walked up to a gift store and ordered some cookware as a gift for the wedding. Sasha then went to another store and purchased a set of pearl jewelry for Vian's mother.

She went back to the flower shop and got the flowers wrapped. Having flowers delivered by some store people on your mother's birthday is an offense. At least for Sasha, it was rude to have someone else deliver flowers to a mother on her birthday.

'Jeez. This man is so cold. Why can't he just visit his mother on her birthday?' She whispered to herself. Another part of living alone is you start talking to yourself.

Sasha took the gifts and flowers, got in a cab, and went to Vian's mother's house which was a twenty-minute drive away. But with the traffic, it took her another thirty minutes.

Sasha got out of the cab and asked him to wait. She would have to return to work afterward. She went up to the house and rang the doorbell.

An older lady opened the door. She was dressed in a peach dress and was in her late sixties or early seventies. She had her hair done and her nails were painted red. She was wearing a pearl necklace and had her makeup on. Sasha was quite impressed by this old lady who was also the mother of her hot boss. She was drooling all over her son.

"Hello. How may I help you?"

"Irani. Right?" Sasha asked with the flowers in her hands.

"Yes. Irani."

"Ma'am, happy birthday. Vian sends these flowers and a present. Sorry, he couldn't make it."

"Oh, thank you, honey. You?" The old lady asked Sasha.

"I am Sasha. Vian's new personal assistant," Sasha handed her the flowers and the present.

"Oh, honey. You want to come in? For a coffee?"

"Actually, can we do it some other time? I have to return to work," Sasha told Irani.

"Of course. I know how cold my son is. And he can get strict. But I also know he would just ask someone to order flowers online. It is nice of you to come in person." She took the flowers. Sasha noticed she was wearing nice jewelry on her arms. Sasha liked those diamond bracelets and gold bangles. Sasha herself came from a nice family, but this? This was epic. How did his mother know he didn't send her to give her the flowers? But that's the mother. She probably was used to getting flowers delivered each year. How dry is this man? So cold. Who gets flowers delivered to his mother? It's a once-a-year event. Mom's Birthday! Cheez.

"Thank you, Ma'am, and have a great birthday," Sasha wished her.

"I have a party on Saturday. I would love to have you join my party. How did he find such a gorgeous personal assistant?" Irani asked Sasha with a smile.

"Thank you, ma'am. You are very generous, and I will try my best," Sasha nodded yes and gave her number to the elder lady.

"Thank you for the invite, Ma'am."

"Oh, call me Irani. Don't be so formal, honey," Irani hugged the girl.

Sasha got in the cab and was on her way to her office.

Chapter – 32

There was silence in the cab. Sasha checked her phone and there were no messages. The driver broke the silence.

"So, you from India? What's your name?" The cab driver was Indian.

"Why do you ask?" Sasha asked him, sitting in the back seat.

"Oh, you look Indian and you sound Indian. So, I asked. I am from Moga," the man with short black hair and dark skin questioned her again.

"I am from India. Delhi. But I am not from Punjab," Sasha tried to ignore the man, but could she?

"Oh, nice. Delhi is nice. Where in Delhi?" The man again questioned Sasha.

"How far are we?" Sasha changed the conversation.

"We have another twenty minutes of drive left. It is rush hour, so hard to get back into the city," the driver said, looking at Sasha through his rear mirror.

"Ok. Thank you." Sasha got on her phone and pretended she was not paying attention. Sasha was deep in her thoughts. How could this world be so dry? How can you not see your mother on her birthday? And she had a crush on this cold man who looks hot?

Her mind was racing. She didn't know how to comprehend all this she was witnessing. She had partied with strangers on a boat, and the days were magical but unexpected. She wasn't hoping for anything. She was just trying to live each day. She was not living in the future or the past. Yet the past was here. She could not still believe she had seen Robin. Robin, the devil in her life.

If she could, she would punch him in the face he thought was so pretty to take advantage of her innocence. She wanted to bruise him. But she was still not sure if it was him she had seen. Or was she reminiscing about him? It was early morning and he had come out of the elevator with many other people.

"Miss, your stop is here," the driver told Sasha. She got out of the cab.

"Thank you," she said as she shut the door.

Sasha was in high heels and a great dress. Her hair was down and it was past afternoon. She still had a lot of work to do.

Sasha walked up to her office building and went to the elevator. She swiped her ID card and got in. She did feel thankful for all that Vian had done for her. Why would some dude just out of the blue give her a job? The job wasn't difficult. Demanding? Yes. Sasha made it to her floor where she was working with a man who was probably a dream to many women.

And nice enough to send a gift to his ex-girlfriend. Sasha wanted to see his ex. She wasn't sure why.

Sasha entered her office and found Vian in his workout shirt running on the treadmill. He had his headphones on and couldn't hear Sasha entering the office. Sasha quietly went ahead and took her chair.

Vian got off his treadmill and wiped his body with a towel. Sasha was sitting at her desk and working on her emails, but could she take her eyes off this man? She probably couldn't. She looked at his topless body periodically. She could notice how well-built his body was, and his stomach had abs. A six-pack. She must not fuck this up. She shouldn't be drooling over her boss. For a lot of reasons.

One of them? She could be fired.

Vian wiped his sweat off with the towel and then put his shirt back on. He went back to his chair and started his work again. This is all the work it takes to get all the gits and glam? Sasha was working on her computer. She got another email and it was from her new hot boss. They were in the same room, but he had sent her a thank you email.

"Thank you for delivering flowers to my mom's place in person."

"You are welcome," Sasha responded as she smiled.

Vian picked up his phone and called someone. Sasha was busy getting through the rest of the emails.

A few minutes later Sasha's worst nightmare materialized.

There was a knock on the door.

"Come in," Vian looked at the door.

It was no one but Robin. Robin walked straight to Vian's desk.

Sasha was at her desk and the only thing she was praying right now was that Robin wouldn't see her. She didn't want to be seen by this man. She was hiding from the whole world under the name of Sasha. She hid from her past, her ex-boyfriend, and her gay ex-husband. Robin was one part of her past. The past she hated. She was angry again. So, she did see this asshole in the elevator. Robin walked up to Vian's desk and shook his hand. Sasha was sitting on her chair watching everything happening in front of her eyes. He was the guy who had used her and left her without any answer. So many lies altogether. She wanted to know why. Why did he leave? Could she ask him? She wanted to ask him but also to punch him in the face.

Had he not left her, she would not have married Jordan who happened to be gay.

Oh God, what was happening? Sasha's mouth was drying up as she tried to hide her face behind her laptop which was not very big.

Sasha wanted to leave the room. She was not able to breathe. She felt suffocated. She felt like someone was strangling her neck with a scarf and she would die. Sasha drank the water in the glass and finished it.

She got up and tried to leave the room.

"Sasha, where are you going? Come here. Let me introduce you to our communication guy," Vian stopped her.

"Oh, sorry. I was just heading to the washroom." She went back to Vian's desk. Robin had his back to Sasha.

"Meet our communication specialist, Robin."

Robin turned his head to Sasha.

"This is Sasha, my personal assistant. She is a new hire," Vian did the introduction.

"Hello," Robin got up and stuck his hand out to shake hands with Sasha.

Sasha stuck her hand out too and shook hands with him. This was the last thing she wanted to do. To shake hands with the Monster. She shook hands with this handsome devil she was in love with once upon a time. A man she gave her whole body to and who was a liar. She felt like someone had electrocuted her. But surprisingly Robin did not recognize her. He had no clue who she was.

"Hello." Sasha pulled her hand back and took the chair.

"Robin was off work a week on vacation. He has just returned. This fella is my main guy. He makes sure we are out there in the media," Vian added to the introduction.

"Sasha, can you please book one more ticket for LA? Robin will be joining us on our business venture."

"Yes, for sure. I will make the arrangements." Sasha said, sitting on the chair next to Robin. Only she knew what was going through her mind right now. Sasha held herself together and acted like she had just met him. Sasha was confused and surprised that a man who had been with her for a few months could not recognize her.

Vian explained the task to both of them, and all three of them returned to their desks. The day was almost done anyway. But Sasha ensured she had all her work assignments done before leaving for home.

She went on the travel page and booked a ticket for Robin. It was a different flight than the one Vian and Sasha were flying on. She would keep this man as far away as she could. She booked him an economy class ticket in a middle seat and at a different flying time.

She would make this man's life hell. At least as much as she could. He didn't deserve to fly in first class anywhere. Plus, you need a class and he didn't have any. Vian was a brand. There was no competition or comparison between them.

Sasha was still trying to wrap her head around this whole situation. She closed her laptop and did a final check on all her work. She grabbed her purse, entered the elevator, and walked out of the door. She wished she could return to Vian's penthouse and get mad at him. But that was not a possibility. He had assigned her a task and she must comply with it.

Chapter – 33

The streets of Vancouver were just gorgeous. But nothing looks beautiful if you don't feel good from inside. She wanted to call someone and tell them she had seen the monster. But who? Who would understand the pain she was going through? She had wanted Robin to be her husband once upon a time. Sasha walked on the street and was thinking. She wanted to scream at the top of her lungs but would get noticed. She couldn't go home and tell her friends.

She would have to share space with a man she hated the most. Robin had lied to her over and over again. Used her, showed her dreams. And then one day disappeared like a dream, leaving Sasha in deep depression.

The city was busy. People were rushing to go home. She had a place to live in, but was that home? Home is where you belong. She belonged to no one and nowhere. Not at this moment. Maybe one day.

Sasha entered a pub. The pub was busy in the evening. You can be in a crowd and still alone. Everyone stopped by for a drink or two before they headed home. She still needed to find a place she could call home.

"What can I get you, miss?" A very handsome Caucasian bartender asked Sasha who had seated herself by the bar on a high stool.

"Oh hi. Can I please start with a beer?" Sasha put her purse behind her chair. She was not too far from her place. She checked on her phone and went on Facebook. She searched for Robin by name. She was never able to find when she looked for him. Now she knew where he was living. She entered his name, and it showed up. His Facebook was pretty private and she couldn't see how many friends he had. But then he had Instagram.

Sasha wanted to destroy this man's peace, but she had no power. She was just an employee like he was. Could she tell Vian? Probably not. Sasha drank her beer. No one in the pub bothered her. She was alone and her mind was all over the place. Should she call Vian and quit the job?

But it was that man she wanted to get rid of, not the job. She was loving her new role. She would not

283

have accepted the offer if she had known that Robin was an employee there. She was still in shock that he did not recognize her. Or maybe he did, but he feared losing his job.

"Excuse me," Sasha called the bartender again.

"Yes. What can I get you?" The bartender asked Sasha.

"Can you please get me the strongest drink you have?" She asked.

"Can I make you double tequila or gin?" The bartender asked.

Sasha read the name tag on his shirt. He was Dominic and he had blue eyes.

"Ok. Thank you, Dominic," Sasha agreed to it, finished the beer, and passed the empty glass. Who would understand her? She was in intense pain. But pain is supposed to be part of growing? She couldn't see any growth in this.

"Can I please get another tequila shot along with my drink?"

"Certainly yes," the bartender got her another tequila shot.

Sasha took the shot and asked for the bill.

"Would you like to try our pizza? It's special today," the bartender asked Sasha.

"Ok. Can I please take it and go and pay my bill altogether?" Sasha wanted to cry. The alcohol in her system was making her emotionally weak. The world must not see tears in your eyes. It's like feeding blood to the sharks. Sasha had learned this a long time ago. Life was itself a school of its kind.

"So, what is your plan for the rest of the evening?" The bartender handed in her bill and a small pizza box.

"Well, I have work tomorrow. So most likely I will go home and sleep," Sasha took the pizza box. The pub was still busy and happening and it was not even the weekend.

"Well, that is a great idea. You have a great evening," the bartender said to Sasha.

"Thank you." She had consumed three shots of tequila and she was feeling it. She was drunk and her emotions were running high.

She opened the door and walked out. The day was still bright. She had to walk two blocks to get to her apartment, where Vian lived.

She wanted to go and tell him everything she was going through, but she couldn't. She was not so drunk as to do such a thing. Plus, he was her new boss. She might get fired. There was no room left to take chances.

Chapter – 34

"Good morning, Sasha. How are you?" The receptionist asked.

"I am doing well, and you Cathy?" Sasha was trying to smile. She knew she now had to deal with her worst nightmare. The devil who raped her over and over again in the name of love. Sasha decided not to quit the job. Vian didn't know all this. Maybe she should tell him. But it was her past and this was a new life and a new job.

"Sasha, we were able to find a spot for you. So, you have been moved from Vian's cabin to a new spot. It's Wing 4 and your cabin is second to the left," Cathy told Sasha.

"Oh. OK. And where exactly would that be?" Sasha looked confused. Plus, she had to move away from Vian.

"Oh, good morning, babe." Just then Robin came up to the desk.

"Good morning, Robin," Cathy smiled.

"Oh, hey babe. How are you doing?" Robin was flirting hard with Cathy and she seemed to be enjoying it.

"I can show you your desk. It's on the same floor as mine," Robin put his hand on her shoulder.

Sasha couldn't say anything. He was a well-built devil. She could notice his biceps popping through his shirt which looked so tight on him. His thick hair had a nice comb over-cut.

"Yes, please. Thank you," Sasha tried to be polite.

The only good thing about this whole situation was that he didn't know who she was. Maybe the way she was dressed and her name were different. Plus, he could never imagine she would be here in Vancouver. Sasha let it flow. She followed him to the elevator and onto the floor she was on. It was one floor below Vian's. She couldn't be in Vian's cabin anymore. Back there, she could watch him all day long. That handsome man so smote her. Once your heart desires someone, your eyes can't see anyone else beyond them. For her Vian seemed to be a perfect man. She snapped out of her thoughts. She had to deal with this monster.

There was silence in the elevator.

"You look very familiar sometimes. It's like I know you," Robin told Sasha.

Her heartbeat rose. Her mouth dried up. She would have to say something.

"There are seven billion people on this planet. I am sure there must be someone who looks like me?" Sasha tried to cut the conversation. Her heart was beating fast. She hated the guy but also loved the job and the man who had hired her. You have to pick your battles. Was he worth a fight and quitting a job? No.

Sasha kept her mouth shut and kept following him. This was the second close encounter.

Possibly the new haircut and the color she had just got done, and the new dresses Vian had got her made a difference. On top of all that he couldn't even imagine her being in Canada. How could that be possible? Sasha had to overcome this fear.

"Here. Looks like this is your new spot, gorgeous," he was not hesitant to flirt again.

"Thank you," she took over her new desk.

"Well, I will leave you alone. If you need anything, call me on my extension *3406." Robin left her.

Sasha heaved a sigh. "Wow, thank goodness whoever invented makeup." She pulled her chair and sat down. Sasha was angry, scared, and confused. She had questions, but they didn't matter. She hated him.

Her desk was in front of the window. She could see a tall building in front of her window. The view was similar to Vian's office, but the cabin size was small. There were two screens in front of her and a keyboard. She also had stationery and notepads on her desk. And a big vase full of red roses. There was a note in the flowers. She took out the note and opened it. It was from Vian.

"Enjoy your new space, Vian."

For a split second, she had forgotten about Robin. But then she got back to it. Robin would get on his knees and say sorry. Had he never loved her?

Sasha opened her emails. She had a confirmation for Robin's ticket in business class as per Vian's instructions. Sasha had a different plan. She wanted revenge.

Sasha logged into the account and canceled the business class ticket for Robin. She then searched and found an economy class ticket. She picked a seat in the middle between two seats.

"It's time. I'll make your life hell, Robin," she whispered to herself and sent an email to Robin. Sasha has the devil in her eyes. She knew karma is a bitch, but it was his turn to suffer. How would she do it? She didn't know, but day by day she would make his life hell. Until he decided to quit!

What could he possibly do? This was not the place where he was her professor. They were colleagues. He could probably never even imagine it was the same naïve girl from the girls' college that he had tempted with dreams and taken advantage of. Sasha ground her teeth. The day for some reason had slowed down. She was all caught up with her emails.

Sasha had not seen Vian all day. She technically didn't need to see him. All the work was done via email. But she got up and walked up to his cabin on the next floor. She wanted half a day off. She needed to put herself together. Plus, she had done all the work.

She knocked on the door.

"Oh, come on in, Sasha," Vian noticed it was Sasha from his glass door.

"I booked the flights. There were no business class seats left for the flight, so I had to book an economy class ticket for Robin," Sasha handed him in the paperwork.

"Unless you want him in business class, I can switch with him and take the economy class. It is no big deal. Or I can try some other flights?"

Vian took his glasses off. He had a little bit of beard and that was nicely trimmed. Sasha looked at him and she just froze. She had a crush on him, but lots of other women probably did too.

"Have a seat, Sasha," Vian took the papers and looked at them.

"You don't have to switch seats. It is first come first served basis. I was not planning to take Robin with me as he was on vacation. But it is good to have our media guy with us. So that he can take care of all the needs required for the advertising," Vian looked at the papers as he spoke.

Sasha smiled in her head. All that she wanted was to make this man's life a living hell. She had booked the hotel, but if she could, she would have installed bed bugs into his bed. Sasha's mind was not focused. She had anger burning in her. She couldn't tell her new boss what had happened. Maybe she should? Maybe get him fired. But that was not an act of revenge. Sasha wanted him to suffer... Like she had.

"Vian, I have finished the work for today and it's 4 pm. You think I could take the day off a little early? I have a little bit of a headache," Sasha asked him.

"Oh yes. Go home and take rest. Let me know if you want to go eat out later. Or you can drop by, or I can," Vian asked as he smiled at her.

"You are so nice. You know you are also my boss?" She asked Vian.

"Yes. And also, your neighbor. I am so lucky to have such a beautiful neighbor," he smiled.

Sasha smiled and blushed. She could sense there was something in his mind. Was he in love with her? Roses in the morning and compliments, and then dinners and lunches? What boss treats their employee like this?

"Thank you for the compliment. Let me see how I feel after a nap," Sasha got off her seat and left the room.

She was still smiling and hoped no one saw her. You only smile by yourself when you are in love with someone. Now she wondered if Vian liked her. He didn't leave out a chance to go out with her. But then she was confused. Why did he switch her desk to somewhere else?

"Oh, men are so complicated." She was walking to her home which was across the road. She looked up in the sky and said it aloud.

She took the elevator and went to her apartment. Sasha was exhausted. When she worked in the café, she could run after work, but this mental exertion was tiring her out. She wanted to sleep. She opened the door to her flat, and suddenly life had some other plans for her.

"Nikki," Sasha screamed as she dropped her purse on the floor. She went to Nikki and lifted her head. Nikki lay on the couch unconscious and her mouth was open and her hand was hanging down limply.

"911. What is your emergency—Police, ambulance, or fire?" Sasha had called 911 and she heard the response from a lady.

"Ambulance. My roommate is not responding. Her mouth is open and she is unconscious."

"OK. Keep her sitting up. We are sending an ambulance," the attendant responded.

Chapter – 35

Nikki sat up, but she could barely open her eyes. Sasha went to the kitchen and warmed some water, put some turmeric powder in it, and gave it to Nikki.

"You know what? I am so mad right now. I want to slap you for doing such stupid things. Now drink this up," Sasha asked Nikki to sip up as she helped her sit up.

A few minutes later the doorbell rang, and Sasha went to the door.

It was the paramedics. It was just fifteen minutes since she called them.

They took Sasha's statement. Nikki was still unconscious. They gave her some sort of injection. Sasha was standing there and watching. The paramedics put Nikki on a stretcher and took her to the ambulance.

Sasha sat there alone. The apartment was empty. She prayed that everything went ok. She tried to call Ira, but her phone went to voicemail as usual. Sasha sat in front of their idol. She had no hunger and her tiredness had been taken over by the worry. Before she even realized it, it was past 6:00 p.m.

Without a second thought, Sasha put her shoes on and went up to Vian's floor. She knew he was her boss, but he was her neighbor first.

The elevator door opened on the penthouse floor. They were friends, right? Sasha was still contemplating her action in seeing her boss, her neighbor. Well, at least she was not drunk this time.

Sasha got out of the elevator. Her heart was beating fast. But her gut feeling was not bad. You should always listen to your gut. Sasha went up to this gigantic double door with a camera installed and rang the doorbell.

She was rubbing her hands together. She didn't know if Vian would get mad at her for showing up this late. They both had work. She didn't know if he was home yet. Vian worked late hours. But he had asked her if she wanted to grab dinner.

She was lost in her thoughts. Just then the door opened.

"Oh, hello beautiful. I thought you wouldn't come. Come on in," Vian held the door open for her. He was indeed just in his towel.

"Sorry. Don't mind me. I just took a shower," Vian told Sasha.

"Sorry I am bugging you at this late hour," Sasha apologized, getting into the house. Again, she was mesmerized by the interior. He had a waterfall in his house.

"No, no, it's all right. I am always home alone at this hour. We can eat together. Let me go and change."

Vian's chest was bare. She liked how this man was so handsome. Sasha could notice his shaved chest and well-built calves. She heaved a deep sigh as he walked toward his room.

Vian returned to the living room, dressed in a white shirt and black shorts. Sasha sat on the couch and was hesitant.

"What would you like to eat?" Vian went into the kitchen and looked in the fridge.

"Well, you are the chef. So, whatever you like? Show me what you can cook," Sasha looked at him and smiled.

"Would you like to have some Gnocchi with Focaccia Genovese?" Vian was looking in his fridge.

"Well. I am not sure what it is, but it sounds delicious," Sasha honestly told him.

Vian poured some wine without asking Sasha and passed it on to her. She smiled and took the glass.

"You don't ever eat anything normal?" Sasha took another sip from her wine glass.

"What do you mean?" Vian also sipped on his wine.

"Like you know, Dal (lentil curry), Roti (bread), Rice, and such stuff?" Sasha took another sip of wine.

"What do you mean? This is normal. It's Italian. It's easy to make after a hard day of work."

"Well. I don't know half the things you say, Vian. You know, I ate calamari the other day? And the whole time I wondered why these onion rings are so chewy." She laughed.

Vian laughed. "They were not onion rings. They were deep-fried squid." He laughed again and took stuff out of the freezer.

"Yes, I know. I found out later. I was buzzed and they tasted good, so I don't regret it," Sasha eased her hold on her glass. There were some nuts in front of her. Vian also gave Sasha some cheese and crackers to eat.

"Can I help you with something?" Sasha got up and went into the kitchen.

"Sure, you can cut some vegetables." Vian passed her the cutting board and some veggies.

"So, you know why I am here again? Very unexpectedly? I am sorry," Sasha washed her veggies and started cutting them. Vian was listening and quietly preparing the food.

"Yes. Go on," Vian said.

"My roommate just went to the hospital. I thought I was going to come home early and rest, but that never happened," Sasha looked up from the cutting board.

"Why, what happened?"

"I don't know. She was unconscious. She ate some white powder. I saw some lines of white powder on the coffee table," Sasha was chopping the veggies.

Vian took her face in his hands and kissed her. She didn't know what to do. Sasha left the knife, turned around, and kissed him back.

There was silence between them. Sasha had no clue what had just happened.

"I like how innocent you are," Vian kissed Sasha again on her neck. She didn't repel or rebel. She was already ready to be broken into his arms. Even though she thought this could never happen, it was happening.

Sasha held Vian from his waist and he held her from her waist. They both were in each other's arms. Breathing and looking into each other's eyes. Vian let Sasha go.

"Your friend did cocaine. She probably snorted through her nose. You don't eat that stuff, silly." Vian took a ceramic pan and put it in the oven.

"Dinner should be ready in 30 minutes. Let's go relax for a bit," Vian wiped his hands and put the cloth back on the stove.

"She will be ok, right Vian?" Sasha was done cutting the veggies.

Vian put his arms around her, moved her hair back from her neck, and kissed her again.

"She will be just fine," he told her as he rocked her in the kitchen.

"So, is this a date?" Sasha was still in his arms.

"Yes. Looks like it is a date with you, my gorgeous love," Vian kissed her again. He poured more wine into two glasses and walked to the living room.

Sasha followed him.

Sasha was smiling. She had drooled over him when he was working out in the office topless or when they went out for lunch. Sasha had many dates with him, but just in her head. She wished someone like him would love her. Now it was happening and she didn't want to jinx it. Sasha and Vian lay on the couch. Sasha lay next to him as they both cuddled. Sasha felt intense peace. What does a woman want? A man with whom she feels secure. She was with a man who not only made her feel secure but also made her feel special. The room was silent. The only voices in there were the sounds of the TV. Just then the oven beeped.

Vian got up, took the food out of the oven, and placed it on two plates. He placed the plates on the dining table and lighted candles in the middle.

"Dinner is now ready, my lady."

"Oh, a man who knows how to make money, is handsome, and can cook food? I must be daydreaming." She smiled and went up to the dining table. Vian pulled the chair out for her.

"Thank you for the compliment," Vian also took a seat.

"Do you have anything bad in you? A dark side?" Sasha asked him.

"Tell me yours and I will tell you mine."

"Well, my dark truth? It is more like a stain than a dark truth."

"Oh yeah? Tell me," Vian took a bite off his plate. Sasha could see his perfectly aligned teeth, his big eyes, and the lashes that were curled up.

"Well, I don't know if it is even worth telling?" Sasha hesitated.

"Come on now, how bad can it be?" Vian looked straight into her eyes.

Sasha who was already mesmerized by this man, felt like a wave of current went down from her heart to the rest of her body.

"I am divorced," Sasha put it out there. They were both eating their meal which was almost done.

"Oh. You poor thing. Who could divorce a gorgeous woman like you?" Vian took her hand in his hands and kissed her on her neck.

"That is sort of irony. He was gay," Sasha allowed Vian to kiss her. She felt again a wave running through her body. She wanted him to take her to bed and make her moan. Sasha was tipsy and she was smiling.

"A gay? Why did he get married then?" Vian moved closer to Sasha and put his hands around her thin waste. He moved her long hair away from her ears with his fingers, and gently kissed her.

"I had no idea he was gay, nor did anyone. Not even his parents." She could barely speak. Vian took her hand and held her in his arms tight.

She picked up her wine glass and finished her wine in one sip. She could feel something was about to happen, but she was not going to stop this. Her gut feeling told her she was secure. She would allow Vian to do whatever he was doing.

"Any dessert, my lady?" He kissed her on her lips.

"You know you are also my boss?" She tried to warn him.

"Yes, and you are my personal assistant. Who is very personal right now." Vian tightened his grip on her waist.

Sasha smiled and eased herself onto his lap.

"So? What is your dark side?" Sasha whispered into his ears.

"I can show you my dark side if you like?" Vian kissed Sasha again on her neck.

"Ok," Sasha agreed.

"You are sure? You want to see my dark side?" Vian asked her.

"Yes." Sasha didn't care. What could be a worse thing she could encounter than seeing her ex?

Vian got up. "You are sure?" He questioned her one more time.

"Yes, I am sure," Sasha was now curious.

"OK. Wait here. Let me prepare it." Vian disappeared.

Sasha got up off her couch and poured some more wine. She had no clue what was about to happen. She was a little nervous but also happy. Was Vian in love with her? Or was he just another guy playing with her? Well, you have to kiss frogs before you find your prince. If he was going to play with her, he was just another frog. Sasha took the dishes and put them in the sink.

Vian came back and put a blindfold on Sasha's eyes.

"Oh. Is it a surprise?" Sasha asked him while he put a cloth on her eyes.

"It is. You can say no anytime and quit." Vian walked her to the bedroom.

"Is it a game?" Sasha was walking as she questioned him.

"Well, it is a game that I like to play with my lover once in a while," Vian took her to the bedroom and made her stand there.

"Are you ready?" He questioned her.

"Yes, I am," Sasha agreed.

Vian took the blindfold off.

"Oh, it's beautiful." Sasha looked at the room full of lit candles. There was a handcuff on his bed.

"You can still say no, Sasha."

"No. Go ahead. I am ready. I am your lover." She looked around. This bedroom she had slept in before didn't look the same.

How much pain could there be? How much could he hurt her? Sasha had been in pain and lonely. She had learned how to live and thrive on pain and hurt. She knew there was only one way after you go down in life... You can only rise up. She liked this man. Vian was so perfect. Would she do this for him? Yes... he made her happy and she was willing to make him happy.

Vian went and turned on his music. He took Sasha to the bed and slowly took her clothes off. She allowed his hands on her. The lights were dim in the room and the music was slow. Sasha sat leaning against the headboard and Vian tied her hands.

Sasha had her bra and panties on.

"Are you nervous?" Vian took his shirt off sitting between her bare legs.

"No. Maybe a little," Sasha let out a deep sigh. He was so handsome and his worked-out body was naked before her eyes.

"We can stop if you want. You don't have to do this, Sasha," Vian unhooked her bra and gently removed it as Sasha lifted her body while her hands were being tied up.

"No. I don't want you to stop. I want to play this game with you," Sasha looked straight into his eyes.

"Ok. Well then..." Vian took a lighted candle, held it over Sasha's body, and poured wax on her belly.

She bellowed in pain. Vian poured some more on her belly... and kissed her on her neck and touched her breasts. Slowly he removed her panties. She had wax on her belly.

"I want you to moan in pain," Vian told Sasha while he held her body against his.

"There is pleasure in this pain." She looked into his eyes.

The lights went dim... there was only music, the candles, the love between them, and two naked bodies breathing rapidly.

Chapter – 36

It was 8:00 p.m. on a weekday night. Ira was outside a Madison hotel in the heart of downtown. She took her cell phone out and made a call.

"Hello," a man's voice.

"Hello. It's me, Ira. Sorry, I am a little early," Ira looked around and the city seemed busy. Several cars were passing, and the day was getting a little dim. It was 7:30 in the evening. Ira was dressed in a short white dress with a deep cleavage cut. She was wearing flat shoes with the dress and was carrying a purse. She opened the purse, took a lip gloss out, and put it on her lips. She then checked if there were condoms in her purse.

She looked at the hotel; it was not ordinary, but quite old. Just then a door opened and a Caucasian man came out. A handsome man, well-built, and with very attractive eyes. Ira loved that arch of his eyebrows. He must be in his early forties. Ira was just twenty-two years old. He said over the phone he liked girls young and tender, and here she was to be with this handsome devil for one night.

"Hello. I am Oliver. Oliver Brodeur." He shook hands with Ira.

"Hi. Sorry, I was supposed to come at 8:00 pm, but I had some time on hand after work, so here I am at 7:30," she walked into the door with him.

"Oh, that is fine. I was alone in the room anyways waiting for you to come."

Ira followed him to the stairs that were carpeted. The walls had antiques on them and very old paintings.

"This is a very classy-looking hotel," said Ira following him. They both were in front of the elevator.

"Wait until you see the room and don't be scared with this elevator. This is very old school and slow, but works fine." He removed a metal rail and then slid the door to the side and they both entered.

"Wow, this is really old school. I have never seen anything like this before." Ira looked at the walls of the elevator.

"Yes, I liked it, so every time I visit the city, I stay here."

They both got out on the third floor.

"Nice," Ira followed him to the room.

"Wait until you go in the room." He opened the door and they entered a classic-looking apartment with a kitchen, a bathroom with a tub, a living room, a dining room, and a bedroom.

Ira walked around and checked the room out. It was indeed a very classic old mini apartment with an ocean view. There were floral couches and printed wallpaper, and the television sitting in a box with doors. She entered the kitchen and noticed a full set of teapots and cups. The pottery was printed with flowers. The retro stove made the kitchen look even more vintage.

"There is wine and beer. What would you like to drink?" The man asked. He had already taken off his shirt.

"I will have a wine. Thank you." Ira put her purse down and sat down on the couch.

"Get comfortable. We have all night." Oliver opened a beer can for himself and sat next to Ira.

"So, you told me you are going to tell me what you do for work in person when we meet," Ira asked, crossing her legs and sipping her wine.

"I did. I am in the business of wine selling. I am originally from Europe." He took his phone out of his pocket and opened his photo icon.

"Look at the wines I sell, and here is my store. I also have some toys. This is a motorcycle I like to ride in summer and this is a car I drive. I also have a truck I use when camping," he scrolled through his photos.

Ira got up, poured some more wine, and took a sip. She came back and sat on the couch again. Oliver was still holding onto his phone.

"I think you have too many clothes on." Oliver put his phone away and moved closer to Ira.

She took her dress off and also her bra. She sat on his lap in her panties.

Oliver held her body tightly and kissed Ira on her neck. He then kissed her on the lips. She let her body loose in his arms. Oliver grabbed her hip closer, got up, and took her into the bedroom.

Ira lay on the bed and Oliver slowly pulled her panties down.

"We can make all your fantasies come true," Oliver said, taking his pants off and getting onto the bed with the completely naked Ira.

"You have so many toys?" She was baffled.

"Yes, I do have a lot of toys," Oliver was cuddling Ira while she asked him questions.

"I am your newest toy, Oliver?" Ira rubbed his chest which was shaved and well-built. She noticed his shoulders were big.

"Yes, you are my newest toy." Oliver stood up against the bed and brought her closer to the corner of the bed.

"This is a nice visual." He kissed her toes and her legs and put them on his shoulder. He gently kissed and rubbed Ira's painted toes.

"Which one is your favorite toy of all? Me or the motorcycle?" Ira asked him while she lay on the bed facing him.

"Well, sweety, both of you sound different." He kissed her on her navel as he went down on his knees.

Ira laughed loud and hard. Oliver laughed with her.

"I need some more wine." She got up and went to the kitchen of this very vintage hotel room.

"Oliver?"

"Yes?"

"Can I ask you something?" She poured some wine and took a sip.

"Sure. Shoot away." He got another beer.

"Am I your first Indian girl?" Ira questioned.

"Yes. You are my first Indian girl." He held her in his arms and kissed her neck.

"I like to please... let me," Oliver took her hand and led her to the bedroom. He closed all the blinds and dimmed the lights. The night was still young. Ira lay naked in Oliver's bed. They cuddled.

"I have all night to make love to you," she touched Oliver's chest and his eyes.

Oliver turned the light dimmer, held her tight, and kissed her lips...

"You make me feel very special," she whispered into his ears as their bodies lay naked.

"I enjoy women's company and it should be respectful. Even if they meet me for one night, I treat them nicely." He kissed her navel.

She moaned in pleasure. They had a full night just to themselves.

Chapter – 37

"Can you please show me one size smaller in this dress?" Sasha was in the clothing store. She had shopping to do. Vian had sent her a memo to take along a cocktail dress on the trip. Apparently, there was an event where she had to go with him. She was excited, but the idea of Robin on the same trip was haunting her. She was sick to her stomach. She had no idea how to get rid of him. Sasha was surprised he didn't recognize her. She hoped he never found out it was her. Everything would be so complicated. And now? When Vian had made love to her? She didn't want him to know about Robin and her. Vian was not just a boss anymore... He was more than a boss. The last thing she wanted to happen was to jinx this perfect fairy tale she was living in. She was still in a state of disbelief. How did she get so lucky with Vian? Yes, it was painful sex.

Sasha had painful sex. She couldn't decide what was more painful. A man who melts warm wax over her body and promises to love her forever? Or a man who played with her in the name of love?

"Try this and let me know if you need any smaller. We also have extra small," the lady just distracted her from her thoughts. Life felt like magic and hell at the same time. She definitely needed to get rid of this man somehow. She would put a bullet through his head if she could, but that was not a possibility. She would end up in jail and her fairy tale with Vian would end before it began.

Sasha took the dress with a "Thank you" and entered the trial room. She put the dress on and got to look in the mirror.

"Oh my. You look heavenly," a man standing there complimented Sasha.

"So, it's a yes?" Sasha smiled at this stranger and asked.

"One hundred percent. Are you taken? Or can I ask you out for a drink tonight?" The man asked Sasha.

Sasha laughed. "Aww. I am flattered, but I have a man," Sasha told him even though she was unsure about Vian's intentions. They had made love to each other, but marriage? That was a hard one.

"Oh... that sucks. All the pretty ladies are taken." The man smiled and walked away. Sasha paid for her dress and then moved to a few more stores. She had a trip coming up. She was excited. No matter what happened, she would not let Robin ruin her life once again.

Sasha had a few bags. She got a cab and made it back to her apartment. Nikki was back from the hospital and Ira was also there.

"Shopping?" Ira asked Sasha.

"Yes, I have a trip coming up. How are you, Nikki? You better now?" Sasha put her bags down.

"Yaa man... I really died. They put me on IV for a night and then kept me in the hospital for a few days," Nikki was smoking again.

"Well, welcome back. Shouldn't you be not smoking?" Sasha asked her.

"I am going to rehab in a few weeks. I should be ok. Dad is really angry though," Nikki smoked and exhaled.

"You found some sort of sugar daddy, Sasha? This is like all the time you are shopping," Ira laughed.

"Shut up, Ira. I am not like you are," Sasha got angry at her comment and taking her bags was about to walk away.

"What do you mean, you are not like me?" Ira grabbed her arm and questioned.

"You are an escort. I saw what was inside that envelope the other day. A note that I read accidentally," Sasha told her, taking her hand off her.

"How can you say that? How dare you?" Ira was angry and held her again and turned her around.

"Take it easy, guys. No fighting or aggression. Take a Toke both of you, have a drink, and call it quits," Nikki sat up on the couch and tried to stop them.

"You are going to tell us, Nikki? You almost died a couple of days ago from a drug overdose," Sasha told Nikki.

"OMG. You are such a judgmental little bitch. Shit happens!" Nikki got up and went out on the balcony.

"People do what they need to do. It's not like you are all clean, Sasha. You have been missing or coming late for so many nights. Little Miss Perfect Angel," Ira was angry.

"I don't sleep around like you do. Some dude just had sex with you in this living room. How much do you charge them? Like seriously, some days I feel like I am living with a drug addict and a hooker," Sasha's face was red with anger. She had no idea how she was saying all this, but something in her made her say all this.

"You know what, Miss Perfect? You wouldn't get a room this cheap for 500$ in the heart of downtown. The minimum it goes for is 1000 dollars and above. You are most welcome to take your ass out somewhere if we are so bad for you," Nikki also jumped into the conversation.

"I can't believe you are saying all this to us, Sasha?" Ira had tears in her eyes.

"Yes, after we partied together and we gave you this makeover. Just look at yourself, Sasha. No one can even recognize you. This head-to-toe look? It's me and Ira. You truly broke my heart and we thought you were part of us," Nikki stood in the room and joined the conversation.

"What about the things you borrowed? We helped you and you are returning all the favors like this? We did it without even knowing anything about you? And this is what we get? You must be out of your mind to talk to us like this," Ira was crying hard now.

"What possibly can turn someone into a hooker?" Sasha stood there with her hands on her waist.

"What's it to you? You have already called me a drug addict and her a hooker. Why does it matter? You know what, sweety, there is a list of girls lined up to get this room so cheap." Nikki was angry.

Ira was standing there and crying. She was sobbing. Sasha was quiet.

"What? Why are you quiet now? Bring on more of your bullshit," Nikki raised her voice. She was angry. She took a glass and threw it on the floor. She went and gave Ira a tight hug.

The living room was heated with the angry conversation. Sasha took her bags, went to her room, and shut the door.

"Yes, go into your fucking room and never show us your face," Nikki told her off.

The apartment was quiet. Everyone was in their rooms and no one was talking.

Chapter – 38

Sasha reached Vian's mother's house. She could hear the sounds coming from inside. Was this a good idea? To show up? Now she was having doubts in her mind. It was Vian's mother's birthday. Her gray hair was elegantly coiffured, and she had worn a nice dress when they first met.

There were black and gold balloons on the side of the door. She was skeptical about going in. No one had seen her walking to the door; she could possibly make a U-turn. Oh well, not really. She just then realized there was a camera at the door. She was in a pink dotted dress. The dress code was to dress like you were in the sixties. She was lost in her thoughts. It felt so wrong right now that she was at the party without her boss. Well, Vian was not just a boss anymore. They made love and went on dates, even though no formal words were spoken about them being in love. Does love need any confirmation? Well, she didn't care. She was going with the flow. This felt so wrong though. She was brooding over all this, and just then the door opened.

"Oh, hello, my child. I am so glad you made it," Vian's mother opened the door.

Sasha went ahead and gave her the flowers she was holding in her hands and followed it up with a hug.

"Happy birthday, Aunty," Sasha kissed her on the cheek.

"Thank you, my love. And please call me IRANI." The mother took Sasha inside the house.

You would think sixty years and older would have nice sixties music on, and would be an elegant party with sober people drinking wine. But this was a real shocker. Vian's mother was dressed in a golden dress decorated with sequins. His dad was also dressed in a suit. Sasha had never met him or heard of him. She was not sure why Vian would hide about his dad or never talk about him. There was no mention of him anyway. Maybe he never had the chance.

"Hello, Sasha. I am Daksh. Vian's dad." The elderly gentleman shook hands with Sasha. Oh, he was so nice. You can sense the vibes of a person. So, this was the dad? Wow, she had finally met the man of the house.

Anyways, Sasha was meeting two lovely humans. She was just standing there enjoying the warm atmosphere and out came this dog, a Pitbull. Black with white paws and a mark on her neck.

"Sasha, come meet our second baby, Panda." Sasha's mother brought the dog closer to her.

Sasha had a special spot for dogs. She had one while growing up, and in just one week, she had fallen in love with the animal. How expressive they are, even without a voice.

"What a lovely dog, Irani!"

A black and white dog. Sasha fell in love with the dog instantly. She bent down and petted the dog. The dog was so excited and wagged her tail and licked Sasha's face.

Sasha could see a couple of other people in the house. The house was big for a house in the city and she felt warm and welcomed. But where was the party? She could hear the music, and the house was decorated with balloons.

"Come sweety. Let's grab a drink," Irani walked Sasha to the backyard after they went through the living room and kitchen.

And there it was. The party was in the backyard. There were tables, a live band, and many people.

"Wow! What a beautiful setup," Sasha addressed Vian's mother.

"Oh, thank you, my love. It is a Greek-themed party. Daksh's friend requested a live band. They are really good," Irani told Sasha as she walked her down the steps to the lit-up backyard.

There was a bar in the corner. The backyard was decorated with balloons and yellow outdoor lights on the trees. High tables were set up and people were standing near them. The high tables had black tablecloths on and some had navy blue covers. There was a bar in the corner where a man was standing and serving drinks.

Sasha again thought she must be in a dream. This was so romantic, and she wished Vian was here for some reason. Maybe she could text him? Maybe he didn't even know his parents were having a party. Maybe he needed to be reminded? Well, she was technically a personal sectary. It was her job to remind him.

Sasha took out her phone, typed the text, and created an email.

"Hello Vian, I think you probably missed the invite to your mom's birthday celebrations at her residence. I am just reminding you.

Sasha,

Personal Secretary"

She hit the send button. She went to the bar and got herself a drink. There was a full table set up with a Charcuterie Board with different types of cheese, crackers, and fruits on it. There was hummus, pitta bread, and all sorts of food. Sasha took some food on a plate and found a table to put her drink on. She seemed a little early, so the party was not that busy.

"Hey, darling! You standing alone?" Vian's dad came around and asked Sasha.

"Oh. I am just really enjoying this food here. I mean who misses this cool party?"

"Well, Vian has been missing these parties for many years now. I guess he loses the invite with all the other emails he receives." Vian's dad sarcastically told Sasha.

"I guess so, sir," she replied.

"Oh, sweety, don't call me sir. Call me Daksh." He rubbed her shoulder.

Sasha smiled.

"Cheers," Vian's dad raised his glass in a toast.

The evening was getting closer to the dark. The live performance by the band was on. Sasha noticed that the backyard was getting full in less than half an hour. She walked around with the glass of wine. She didn't have a plan to drink a lot. This was not her apartment or Vian's penthouse. This was his parents' place. How cool they were! Sasha thought of her parents for a second. She had tears in her eyes. She changed the thought.

"Hey, Sasha." Someone just tapped her shoulder. Oh, it was Vian with flowers. She had just sent him an email a few minutes ago. Had it been that long? She really must be lost in this amazing moment.

"Oh, you made it?" Sasha wasn't expecting him to be here at the party. She wanted to just send a reminder and not feel guilty for attending her boss's parents' birthday party when he was not there. She knew the city was dry and people were cold. But not this much that they would miss special events like this.

"Yes indeed. Thank you for reminding me." He gave her a kiss on her ear hidden under her hair. Sasha looked at him in surprise. She noticed that his parents were observing Vian kissing Sasha and hugging her. Daksh was smiling.

Lost in her thoughts she could feel Vian was in love with her. Why were there so many lunch dates? He didn't take anyone else for a lunch date. It was usually her.

Vian went to get some more food for Sasha.

"You must be his special girl," Daksh whispered to Sasha.

She looked at him and smiled. She was blushing.

Vian came back with the food. "Babe, let's eat."

Sasha had already had some food. But she did not refuse. This was a truly magical moment. She was meeting his parents and they seemed to like her. Sasha ate from the same plate as Vian.

"You two look so adorable," Vian's mother said while walking by. She passed them a drink. The live band was getting loud. The night was still young and everyone was slowly rocking to the music. And Sasha? She was drunk even without any alcohol.

The night was beautiful and she loved the music, the people, and Vian's presence at the party.

Chapter – 39

Vian drove back to their building. It was just 9:00 p.m.

"Babe. We have a flight to catch tomorrow morning. You want to come over to my place before you go to your apartment?" Vian parked his jeep in the underground parking at the spot that was assigned to him.

"Sure," she nodded in a yes.

Vian and Sasha got out of the Jeep.

"Remember we first spoke by the garbage can?" Sasha pointed to the bin in the corner.

Vian laughed. "Yes, I remember. I found love in a hopeless place…" he sang and picked Sasha up. Sasha kissed his face.

"Vian," she said.

"Yes," he replied.

"I want to make you sit down in front of me and kiss your face all day," she whispered in his ears.

"Oh yeah?" He kissed Sasha again.

Vian walked to the elevator. Sasha put her arms around his neck. They both went up to the penthouse floor.

Vian and Sasha went in and sat on the couch. Vian held Sasha's feet up and took her shoes off. Then he massaged her feet as she lay on the couch. They both cuddled and kissed.

"I love you, Sasha." And there it was. The words she wanted to hear.

"I love you too, Vian." She hugged him tightly and then got off the couch. "I have to go home and pack."

"Sure," he let her get out of his arms.

Sasha kissed Vian, shot out of the door, and went to her apartment. There was a happiness that was surrounding her.

There was silence in the apartment. It felt like someone had died. She was familiar with this silence. She felt it when she was at home. Sasha lay on her bed. She had just got mad at her roommates. Nikki might ask her to leave. She would have to find a new place to live. But she was OK. Vian paid her well. The future was uncertain again. There was a monster at her work she didn't want to deal with. She was surprised he had not recognized her. She had just had a new hairstyle and new makeup. It wasn't like she had plastic surgery done. Or maybe she had a different name now, and she dressed differently? But Sasha knew every inch of Robin's body. She knew how he walked and once upon a time had been hypnotized by his eyes and spellbound by his words. But you ask her today? She couldn't believe she was in love with this man and had given him all without worrying about the consequences. Should she tell Vian?

Now Vian was her boyfriend. He must know. Sasha had a million thoughts in her mind. But she had also just messed up. She had to fix the mess she had just created. God, how did she come down to this?

Life was so confusing. She worked with her ex-boyfriend while she was in love with her new boss who happened to be Robin's boss too. She would have to tell this to Vian. Vian must know. This was serious. Vian and she had just made love. But before all that she must fix the mess she had created at home.

Sasha sat on her bed and tried to think how she could talk to her roommates. She had messed up. Instead of being grateful for their help, she had sabotaged everything. She should have just shut her mouth instead. What had got into her? Sasha was lost in her thoughts.

When Nikki was home, there was usually music on, but today, everyone was home, and still, it was so quiet. Sasha must fix this. But then, she had a trip coming up. Maybe she would come back and fix this mess. Hopefully, things would calm down by then.

Sasha had to leave early for her work trip the next day.

There was a knock on the door. She opened the door and it was none but Ira.

"Can I come in?" Ira asked Sasha.

Sasha didn't say anything but held the door wide open. Ira got into the room and sat on the bed.

"Before you say anything, I am sorry," Sasha told Ira.

"Well, you are not wrong. I didn't realize when I turned into an escort," Ira told her.

"Sasha, I came to this world and saw brands and lights and shine and I was offered things and money, so I took it." Ira had tears in her eyes.

"Tell me what you would do if you were in my shoes," she asked.

Sasha remained quiet. She was confused. She knew she had hurt Ira. Sasha should not have said those words. Now she was regretting every single second of that moment.

"You know, now I am addicted to this. I can never go back to being regular," Ira was still talking and started to cry. She carefully wiped the tears around her fake lashes. Ira had no makeup on, but her tears were coming down wiping the left-over eyeliner on her face that didn't get cleaned even after a possible makeup remover application. Sasha was standing in shock that Ira was admitting to all this. Sasha still had no say. They both were sitting on her bed. Sasha held Ira in her arms and hugged her.

"You know, Sasha, I am on a student visa and we are allowed to work only twenty hours per week, and that too on a minimum wage. How do you support yourself? This was an easy way." Ira was now crying.

"It's ok. You can always make a switch back." Sasha had her clothes out on the bed and had to pack for a trip. But this, right now, was more important than anything else.

"Sasha, it's not that easy. I send money to India too and my parents are so happy," she said.

"Yeah they are, but if they find out how you make this money? You think they will be happy?"

There was silence between them. Sasha still had tears in her eyes. It was like Sasha had drawn a line and couldn't say anything after that.

"Ira, life is not a bed of roses. We all have our share of problems. But we shouldn't just surrender to the circumstances. You know Diamonds are a compressed form of carbon? Which tells me that even a diamond which is just a form of carbon has to go through immense pressure to form into the most expensive substance in the world. We are humans with minds. We should never give up," Sasha who had learned life through pain, had also formed a great deal of resistance.

Ira got off her bed and walked out of the door after giving her a tight hug.

Sasha started to pack her suitcase. She put in some dresses and some other daily wear clothes. It was a week-long trip in LA. What possible meeting could last for a week? Sasha had no clue. She didn't know what to expect. She was going with the flow.

Sasha decided to stay in her room for the rest of the day. Early in the morning, she would have to leave. Sasha lay on the bed. Sometimes the words should just stay in the mind and not come out of the mouth. Also, what is the point of saying something you know will cause problems in a relationship? Sasha was feeling awful. One suitcase was ready. Sasha's eyes started to close and she fell asleep while thinking of the mess she had created. She had no clue how she would clean it up.

It was 6:00 a.m. and the alarm rang. Vian had booked a cab for both of them. Her heart was beating fast. The feeling was a little different after the night when she was over to his place and they had made love. She knew Vian was more of her boyfriend and lover than just a boss.

The phone beeped. It was Vian's message.

Cab is here. Come downstairs.

Sasha took her bags and went to the elevator. She met Vian in the lift. He hugged her and kissed her on her forehead.

They both got into the cab and were off to the airport.

Chapter – 40

Sasha was sitting next to Vian in the cab. Vancouver Airport was just twenty minutes away from their apartment. The cab was quiet. Both Sasha and Vian were silent, but this silence had peace of some sort. Vian looked at Sasha, held her hand, and kissed it. She smiled.

The driver cut through the morning traffic. Vancouver was a monster of car rush in the mornings. Especially at 6:00 a.m., there was bumper-to-bumper traffic. They would still make it on time because the flight was at 8:00 a.m. Sasha was excited. She had never been to LA and also, she was with the man she was in love with. But she would have to tell him about Robin. That was a bit more complicated.

Sasha was debating in her mind if this was even important. Robin didn't even recognize her anymore. Should she be considering him at all? She needed to move on. And even if he found out that she was Tara and not Sasha? How did it matter? Vian was his boss and he couldn't touch her anymore. Sasha smiled. She truly felt safe with this man. A woman wants to feel safe with her man more than to have money or power. And Vian was such an amazing man she had just landed on.

Sasha was looking out of the window. She saw lights from the buildings making a reflection onto the river. The fresh wind blew over her face and hair. Vian looked at her without her noticing. Soon the cab stopped at the YVR and they both got off. She didn't have to worry about Robin. She had booked him an economy class ticket on the 9:00 a.m. flight. She smiled. A little revenge she had taken. She wanted to destroy his peace. But she also had to work with him. Sasha secretly prayed Robin never found out it was her, Tara.

She should be the one exposing his real side to the world. But now in this time and date, she was the one hiding.

Sasha and Vian entered the airport. Both took in their luggage and checked in. Ahh! Sasha was in a completely relaxed mode. Robin would be on the other flight an hour later than them. She was the one who had booked his flight.

"We have a meeting as soon as we get off the airplane," Vian looked into Sasha's eyes. She was not sure what that was as he smiled.

Life was flipped upside down or downside up for Sasha. A few months ago, she had no place to live, no one to call her own, and no security or assurance she would have a good job. And right now? She had everything. Even a man she thought she could never have. Maybe this was all a dream? Limousine, a penthouse boyfriend who was an Executive Producer, and now a flight to LA in business class?

Had she hit the jackpot? And then she smiled... the evil Robin was not flying with them. She had made sure of that. They checked in their luggage. Sasha was about to see what the business class looked like. Sasha's excitement right now was out of the roof. She couldn't tell Vian. But she was definitely loving him by her side.

After the check-in from YVR, Sasha and Vian were all set to board. The first class and the business class go in first followed by the rest of the people on the plane. They both walked into the business class. Sasha remained quiet as she entered the business class. Oh, there were chairs, not the usual seats. Vian and Sasha's seats were side by side. Her heart was beating fast. She had just made love to the man she worked with, and she was flying with him.

"Babe. Take a seat and relax," Vian took his glasses off and sat down. Sasha was still checking out the business class seating. She had ample legroom and a wide-open space with complementary goodies on the table. You know how a little kid gets excited when he gets a new toy? That was how Sasha was feeling right at this moment.

But she hid it all and kept her excitement to herself. People were walking by. It seemed like this was just the beginning of all her new adventures with this amazing man Vian. Sasha relaxed in her chair in the business class and sipped on the mimosa served to her while the rest of the people were boarding. Just then what she could never expect, her worst nightmare hit her!

"Hello, Senorita." It was none other than Robin.

Sasha, who had booked the flights for all of them was in shock.

"Hey buddy, you made it. I thought you were on another flight," Vian got up and shook his hand.

"I was able to find a last-minute deal." Robin took his LV bag off his shoulder and put it in the cabinet above his seat.

"Oh hey. Great you made it," Sasha had no choice but to smile. But in reality, she was cringing.

She was still glad Robin didn't know who she was. But her plan had just failed. She wanted to punish this evil man. She should tell Vian everything. But then she could possibly ruin her relationship with him too. And now that she was in love with Vian, she couldn't take chances again. She couldn't let this man ruin her life one more time.

She ground her teeth and took a deep breath. Why didn't this man let her live? She was about to have some romantic time with her newest and hot and successful boyfriend in the air. Where no one was there to bother both of them. But not anymore.

Just then the air hostess made an announcement, and everyone had to put their phones away and take their seats.

Chapter – 41

The plane took off. Suddenly, the life that Sasha thought was perfect turned into a nightmare. Her every plan was falling apart. She was silent.

"Everything OK?" Vian questioned her.

This was the first time she was taking a flight in business class. But whenever Sasha tried to have life her way, someone just ruined it. This time it was Robin again.

"Oh yes. Everything is fine," Sasha hid her emotions. But how long could she hide this from Vian, now her boyfriend? At times you want to trust everything, and the next minute you have no one. You stand alone. She didn't know Vian well enough.

She didn't know how he would react to this.

She shook her head and tried to enjoy the amazing flight she was on. Her hair was tied in a ponytail. She took the hairband off and let her hair down. She put her fingers through her hair. Robin was just two seats away from Sasha. She glanced at him, and he was sipping his scotch flirting with the air hostess.

'Pig,' she thought. Sasha was even more angry. If only she could scream, she would tell the world that Robin was nothing but a playboy. Why was Sasha bothered if Robin, her ex-boyfriend meant nothing to her? Sasha had her love sitting next to her. She looked at him and heaved a sigh. How could she switch this situation? Did she fear Robin? No. It was he who had left her. She was lost... and she had just found herself, or she was just finding herself.

Sasha's mind was again racing. How did he make it to the business class? She scratched her head. Vian was busy reading a magazine. He could barely notice anything. Sasha had to come up with some idea to annoy this man. She had an idea. Her eyes shone.

She got up and went to the snack bar.

"Oh, Sasha, you need something?" Robin saw her getting up from her seat and asked.

"Oh, just going to the washroom," Sasha walked to the aisle and used the washroom. Robin who has the aisle seat, looked at her...

Sasha walked back with a glass of juice. She tripped over and the juice fell on Robin.

"Oh, I am sorry," Sasha apologized and looked at Robin.

"Let me get you some tissues," Sasha told him.

"It's ok. I will get it myself." Robin's pants had juice all over them.

Robin left his seat and went up to the galley where Sasha was getting some napkins.

She turned around and gave all the napkins to Robin. He took the napkins and wiped the juice off, but now the stain was on his white shirt. He was wearing a necklace and both his arms were tattooed. Sasha didn't pay any attention and walked back to her seat.

Robin ground his teeth and said nothing. He looked at Sasha walking back and taking her seat.

Vian was checking his emails. Sasha looked at him. He had his glasses on. Sasha put her hands into Vian's hair and kissed him on his ear. He continued to check his emails. Your body gives you a vibe. Her body burned in anger when she looked at Robin, but when she looked at Vian, she felt peace... her body felt calm. There was a peace in which they both belonged to each other. Sasha sat back and took a sip of her champagne.

Just then there was an announcement that they were landing in LA in thirty minutes. The air hostess asked everyone to take their seats and put their seat belts on.

Sasha looked at Robin and he was busy putting his belt on. She wondered if he knew she had thrown the juice on him intentionally. If she could, she would put hot boiling coffee between his legs and damage his balls. But not much she could do.

Or maybe she could? Robin was done putting his seat belt on and looked at Sasha. She turned to Vian and kissed him on his lips. Then she looked back at Robin who tried to pretend he never saw her kissing and focused on the magazine.

What was the best revenge on a man? To see him get hurt? Or to see him helpless?

The plane landed at the Los Angeles airport. A hub for Hollywood celebrities. Sasha walked out of the airplane with Vian and Robin. Robin walked with Vian as he discussed the rest of the week. Sasha was behind them with her carry-on luggage. She was the one who had booked everything. They were all staying at the same hotel.

All three exited the terminal and entered the LAX airport's arrival lounge. The busiest airport in the world. Sasha focused on Vian and wished again they could lose Robin behind.

"Babe. Can we please make a stop?" Sasha asked Vian.

"Oh yes. What do you want?" Vian asked Sasha.

"Well. I just need to go to the washroom," Sasha made an excuse.

"Robin, you go get the taxi and go to the hotel. I will meet you there," Vian instructed Robin. The only thing Sasha wanted. She smiled in her mind.

"Yes, sure. I will meet you guys there. We have a meeting in two hours, Vian," Robin reminded him.

"Yes, sure. I remember. You will need a shower. You have stuff all over you. Let's get you a bib next time," Vian made fun of him and laughed.

Sasha raised her heels and hugged and kissed Vian while Robin was still there. Then she gave her handbag to him and went to the washroom. Robin took his luggage and walked out of the airport.

Just what she wanted. Sasha was again successful in sending Robin away from them. But how long could she do that? She needed a permanent solution to have this monster removed from her life. Sometimes it feels like the whole world is like a forest and there are foxes and other animals everywhere hiding under the human skin. And it gets difficult to protect yourself when you can't figure out what type of animal you will encounter under the human skin. This one? Robin? Was a clever fox! And Sasha was ready to take him down. Her demons wanted revenge, but how was the only question. She believed the whole universe was on her side. She believed she would have justice served! Otherwise, why would she meet Vian? And why would he fall in love with her? There was something above her, and she had faith in those superpowers. Sasha washed her face and got out of the washroom. She took her carry-on bag back and held Vian's hand. They both walked out of the LAX airport and got in a taxi.

Chapter – 42

The driver loaded the luggage in the taxi and Sasha sat next to Vian. She leaned her head on his shoulder. Vian held her hand and kissed her.

The cab was going toward their hotel. Sasha had never been to LA earlier. The roads were wide and surrounded by palm trees. The sky was clear, but the roads were busy. There was silence in the car.

Sasha broke the silence. She desired Vian and he was next to her.

"So, what work do I have here, Vian?" She looked at him and questioned.

"I just wanted you to be with me, babe. Plus, for now, let's just keep it secret." He held her hand and kissed her. Then he kissed her on her forehead.

"And you kiss me so much," she smiled.

"Well, you are too kissable. So, I kiss you." He kissed her again on her cheeks.

Sasha laughed this time. How can someone love you so much? Well, she had loved Robin like this. She had wanted to sit in front of him all day and kiss him as much as possible. Until he disappeared. Maybe she should tell Vian about Robin? Sasha had her mind elsewhere. Robin, her ex who appeared like a nightmare in her life that looked perfect right now. She wished she could get rid of him somehow. She was angry and frustrated. Vian put his arms around Sasha and she snapped out of her thoughts.

She smiled. "I have two different rooms booked for us," she told him.

"That's fine. You can always crash in my room whenever you want," Vian whispered into her ears.

"Yes. I can. Like I do at your place?" She smiled.

The taxi was driving through the roads of LA. Sasha looked outside the window. Life at that moment felt perfect. Minus the presence of Robin.

"You know, that was very nice of you to attend my mom's birthday and send me a reminder," Vian said to Sasha.

"I just did the job of a personal assistant, sir," she smiled at him.

"Silly. You are also the love of my life," Vian kissed Sasha again. She smiled and kissed him back. Soon they reached their hotel and checked in.

Sasha went to her room which was next to Vian's. Robin was on a different floor. Sasha had made a special request to the hotel staff to book Robin's room on a different floor. She had made sure he was not anywhere near them. She had no powers to fire him, but she had the power to keep him away from them. She would have this man booked in another hotel if she could.

Sasha and Vian got settled in their rooms. Vian's phone rang and it was Robin.

"Let's go. We have a meeting in half an hour. You know LA traffic?" Robin told Vian.

"Yes. Meet you in the lobby," Vian hung up the phone and went to see Sasha in her room.

"Babe. I have made some plans for tonight. Just be ready. I should be back in a few hours," Vian kissed her on her forehead and left.

Sasha blushed. She sat on her bed and looked through her phone. She had Vian's mother on her Facebook. Looking through the photos she came across a photo of Avik and herself. How life just appears unintentionally? The only thing that mattered was who you were surrounded with. Right now, Sasha was in the Vian zone and she was loving every little bit of it.

Her phone was ringing. It was Nikki.

"Hello," Sasha took the call.

"Just because I tell you to find a new place, you leave?" Nikki had anger in her voice.

"I am in LA. I didn't leave. But I am sorry for whatever happened," Sasha told Nikki over the phone.

"It's ok. You are somewhat right. I'd rather have an honest friend than someone fake telling me how perfect I am. At least that's what they tell me," Nikki laughed over the phone.

"No. I should have been better than that. I am guilty," Sasha admitted.

"OK, OK. It's all good. I thought you left, that is why I was just checking on you. I come home and usually see you hanging out in your room," Nikki laughed again.

"I didn't mean to say those words. I am sorry," Sasha apologized again.

"It's ok. Why are you in LA?" Nikki questioned.

"I am here with Vian for his work," Sasha told her.

"Oh, your rich lover boy?" Nikki laughed.

"You are silly," Sasha shyly denied, but she knew Nikki was right.

"Ok. You have fun with your lover boy. And we make peace," Nikki responded.

"Thank you." Sasha wanted to tell her what she was dealing with right now. But before she could say anything, Nikki had some news for her.

"So, when are you back?" Nikki questioned.

"I should be back in one week," Sasha replied.

"Well, babe. I won't be here when you get back," Nikki told Sasha.

"Where are you going?" Sasha had a question. She went and looked out of the window.

"I am leaving for my rehab. Dad wants me to go there for three months," Nikki told Sasha over the phone.

"That is a good thing. I am happy for you. Focus and get better. We love you, Nikki. I love you. You are like my sister," she said to Nikki.

"Yes. Sister from another mister." They both laughed over the phone.

"See you when you come back and we will all celebrate," Sasha told Nikki.

"Can't wait, Babe. You have fun and take care," Nikki hung up the phone.

Sasha was alone in the room smiling. The rising sun was an answer to the darkness of the night… There is always hope. She unpacked her things and got a dress out. She was ready for what Vian had planned.

Wasn't she the personal assistant? Then she smiled. She was more than a personal assistant. The day was about to get better. At least, that is what she was hoping for. She went to the bed and lay down on it; before she knew it, she had passed out.

Was this a dream? She wished she would never wake up!

Chapter – 43

There was a knock on the door. Sasha woke up from her nap when she heard the sound of knocking. She went and opened the door.

"Oh, hey gorgeous," Vian held Sasha by her waist and kissed her. Her hair was messed up. It was almost 5:00 pm. Sasha had peace written all over her face. It seemed like all her ducks were in a row.

As he walked into the hotel room, Vian picked her up and shut the door with his leg. He kissed her again and put her on a couch.

"Wow. The very serious-looking man? Can be this romantic?" Sasha sarcastically played with him as she kissed him back. She had her arms around Vian's neck.

"You are light like a feather, my lady. I could carry you to the moon," Vian replied.

He was a dream romantic partner she could not even imagine. She was unsure what was happening, but she loved this.

"You said you have plans? I am hoping something romantic?" Sasha questioned him as she got off the couch.

"Yes. I do. But not romantic. It's a business meeting. That's why you are here." Vian sat on the couch.

"Business? I have to go somewhere with you?" Sasha questioned him.

"Babe. Dress up business. You packed a business suit?" Vian asked her.

"Yes. I did. Let me just get ready." Sasha walked up to the closet to get her suit.

"Great. The meeting starts in an hour and a half in the hotel conference room," Vian told Sasha.

Sasha had her suit in her hands. She was still in a pajama and a T-shirt.

"I am going to the meeting with you?" Sasha questioned again.

"Yes. I need your assistance there." Vian smiled at her.

"Do I need to bring something? I am confused, Vian. I just do things that you ask me to," Sasha confronted him.

Vian held her by her waist and kissed her again on her neck.

Sasha pushed him away. "Vian," she struggled to get out of his arms. Vian was not letting Sasha out of his grip.

"Vian. Love aside? But this is work. Please give me more details. I need to be prepared. I don't like surprises," Sasha got angry at Vian.

"You trust me?" Vian asked, kissing her.

"Yes, I do. A man who lets me sleep in his bed without knowing me? And doesn't touch me? I trust that man," Sasha closed her eyes and kissed Vian on his lips.

"Well, gorgeous. Then get ready. Life is about to change." Vian released Sasha from his tight grip with one more kiss.

Sasha was more than confused, but happily moved toward the lavish shower of the luxury room in the heart of downtown. It felt like some movie. Sasha was falling in love with this man a little more every day.

"Sasha, I'll see you soon downstairs. I have to go instruct Robin," Vian told Sasha.

'Oh yes. How can I forget about this monster.' Sasha put both hands over her forehead. She found herself in a tricky situation where Vian was the present and she had a complex history with Robin. Once a romantic relationship turns bitter, it is simmering to have revenge. But then no revenge is the best revenge. Sasha had to just put Robin on her ignore list and she was good. Not that he knew who she was anyway.

Sasha dressed up in a pink silk pencil skirt dress with white heels. She wore a bracelet that Vian had given her. She put her makeup on and did her hair. She was nervous. She had no clue what she was going to a meeting for, dressed like this.

There was vodka in the room which seemed like a good idea to calm her nerves. Sasha took two miniature bottles out of the fridge and drank them. Oh, the taste was bitter. But who cares? She had to deal with people. Sasha walked out of her room and met Vian in the conference room.

"Oh, hello, my lady," Vian took Sasha's hand and walked her into the room.

There were other people in the room including Robin. Sasha ignored him, walked with Vian, and sat beside him. The conference room had about ten more people.

"Hello everyone. Thank you for flying to LA this evening. I have an important announcement to make," Vian stood before the LED screen as he started his speech.

There was a large wooden table in the middle and there were leather chairs around the table. Everyone was listening to Vian.

"We have a new member we are adding to our company's Board of Directors," Vian looked at Sasha.

"Meet Sasha. She will be our new member on the Board of Directors."

Vian asked Sasha to stand up. Everyone welcomed Sasha with claps.

Sasha was nervous, but the vodka was also working. She was stunned by what Vian had just said. She was being promoted from personal assistant to director on the company's Board. But she had no clue what she would be doing. Her head spun, yet she picked up courage and stood up for a speech.

"Thank you for this new role, Vian. I will try my best to work toward the company's goals."

Sasha was angry, excited, confused, and happy all at once. She wanted to get mad at Vian for not telling her but also loved him for making her feel so special. Robin was also in the same room. Sasha glanced at him. Robin was looking at Sasha and clapping with all the others.

"Everyone, let's meet for cocktails and dinner at the lounge." Vian, dressed in a suit, walked out with some people who surrounded him right after the announcement.

Sasha was also surrounded by many people. All of a sudden, she was the most important person in the group. Sasha was smiling and looking at Vian.

Chapter – 44

As Sasha and Vian stepped into the opulent venue, they were immediately enveloped in an atmosphere of sophistication and glamour.

"Welcome to an extraordinary evening of elegance and indulgence at a cocktail dinner party in the heart of Los Angeles, my lady," Vian walked with Sasha and held onto her hand.

Sasha looked around and noticed that the spacious ballroom was adorned with exquisite floral arrangements, sparkling chandeliers, and tastefully decorated tables covered in crisp white linens.

"You planned this," Sasha was still stunned.

"Yes ma'am. I sure did," Vian smiled.

"Vian. I am supposed to be planning and arranging things for you," she looked at him.

"Well, looks like I have to hire someone else for that job since you are on the Board of Directors." He laughed and gave her a tight hug. He walked toward the rest of the crowd

Soft, ambient lighting cast a warm glow over the room, creating an intimate ambiance that set the stage for an unforgettable evening.

The air was filled with lively conversation and the tinkling of glasses as guests mingled and exchanged pleasantries. Everyone was dressed in their finest attire, the attendees exuding style and grace, adding an air of sophistication. Sasha knew no one but her lover and her destroyer.

The menu was a culinary masterpiece, showcasing a fusion of flavors from all over the world. There were delicate canapés featuring caviar and smoked salmon to succulent miniature beef sliders with truffle aioli. Everyone was enjoying the music. Sasha had a million thoughts running through her mind. She didn't have any hunger. She walked by the bar that offered an extensive selection of premium spirits, champagne, and signature cocktails, artfully prepared by skilled mixologists.

"Can I get you something, ma'am," the server asked, seeing Sasha standing by the bar.

"Can I please get a drink," Sasha asked.

"What sort of drink would you prefer?" The bartender asked.

"Make me anything that would make me drunk."

There should be happiness, but Sasha was a bit stressed. There was Vian who loved her so much, then she just got a new job as a member of the Board of Directors, and then there was Robin she needed to figure out. The tension in her mind was building.

Vian got busy talking to people. Sasha finished one glass of champagne and got herself another one. She definitely was in a dream. This couldn't be real.

The hotel's attentive staff circulated throughout the room, offering trays of delectable hors d'oeuvres and expertly crafted cocktails, tantalizing the taste buds with each bite and sip.

"May I dance with you," a random guy dressed in a white suit asked Sasha.

"Sure," she put her glass away and went on the dance floor.

The evening was filled with gentle melodies of live jazz. The dance floor was adorned with couples swaying to the rhythm of the music. Sasha was in someone's arms dancing. Robin and Vian were both engaged in conversation. Sasha looked ahead and saw her angel and a devil under one roof. As the night progressed, a sense of camaraderie and enmity surrounded her. How would she confront Robin, or should she? When he didn't even remember who she was? But she did. She remembered every second of that time she was with him. She was dancing, but her mind was elsewhere. Robin's presence was suffocating.

Sasha was dancing this gorgeous evening away. Robin stepped on the floor. "May I dance with you?" He asked Sasha.

"Sure," Sasha had no choice. Now Robin's hands were all over her body once again. If she could, she would puke. But right now, she had to suppress it.

The cocktail dinner party should become an unforgettable memory with each passing hour. But a night of elegance, laughter, and indulgence became poison while Sasha was in Robin's arms. Robin didn't say a word. The tension was rising in Sasha. She excused herself and went to the washroom. She looked at herself in the mirror and fixed her hair.

"The show must go on. Sasha, there is no room for emotions. He is just the past,' she whispered to herself. She gathered herself and went out again to the party.

The lobby was full of people. She went and stood next to Vian. She was the new member of the Board of Directors. She must be at her best behavior.

"You are ok, babe?" Vian asked Sasha as she held on to his arm.

"I am ok. I think I am going to call it a night. You can stay if you want?" Sasha questioned Vian.

"No. No. I will come with you." Vian shook hands with everyone and walked out with Sasha.

"Can I sleep in your room?" Sasha asked Vian.

"You need to ask me that? Of course, you can." He kissed her forehead as they both took the elevator to Vian's suite. Vian held Sasha tight as they waited to get out of the elevator.

Sasha took her clothes off and hopped in the bathtub. Vian followed her to the bathtub...

Chapter – 45

Sleeping under the white sheets, Sasha and Vian were all curled up into each other. It was morning. Vian kissed Sasha on her head and put his fingers through her hair.

"Good morning, gorgeous," Vian put his arms around Sasha and held her tight. She was breathing in his closed arms and their naked bodies were wrapped close to each other.

"I love you so much, Sasha," he fixed her hair while her eyes were still closed.

"Vian," Sasha opened her eyes and looked at him.

"Yes." He held her in his arms.

"I want to tell you something. I don't want to start something so big on a lie." Sasha was in Vian's arms.

"Go on." Vian put his finger through Sasha's hair.

"Vian. Can you please be serious and listen to what I have to say?" She took his hand off her hair and looked straight at Vian.

"Baby. We are cuddling and we just woke up. Is it a bad dream or something you want to tell me?" He kissed her on her lips. Vian could not keep his eyes off Sasha. Her beautiful black long hair lay loose on the silk white pillow.

"It is like a bad dream, but is real. If I don't say it now, I won't ever be able to say it again. I don't want to be in a whirlpool of emotions for the rest of our lives." She sat up as she spoke. She covered her bare chest with a sheet.

"If it has something to do with your past, I don't really care. But it is important for you, so go on, babe." Vian put his hands behind his head as he leaned onto the headboard.

"Robin is my ex from when I was in India and everyone knew me as Tara." She looked at Vian.

"Oh. Robin is your ex-gay husband? I was not aware Robin was gay. He has been working with me for just over a year now." He laughed.

"It's not funny. And no, he is not my ex-husband. He is my ex-boyfriend from India." She crossed her fingers and prayed.

"And? What is the problem?" He questioned.

"We work together," Sasha looked at Vian, still looking confused.

"Did he mention something?" Vian asked her.

"He doesn't even recognize me or he is pretending. It is scary. I don't know what is brewing in his mind." Sasha covered her naked body with a blanket. Vian's bare chest was visible and the rest of his body was under the white silk covers.

"You are just overthinking. Forget about it and let's get ready for today's yacht party," Vian brought Sasha closer to himself, hugged her real tight, and kissed her on her lips.

"Get ready, miss member, Board of Directors." He got out of the bed and got into the shower.

Sasha wrapped herself in the robe and went back to her room where her luggage was. She dressed her best for a day on a yacht.

Sasha, Robin, and Vian were aboard a luxurious yacht, a setting that exuded luxury and indulgence. However, beneath the surface of this extravagant scene, emotions were running high, tangled in a web of love and revenge. Sasha didn't know how to let go of the idea of Robin being there. How come he had not reacted? Had he forgotten her? They had had sex many times. Sasha's heart was pounding with a mix of excitement and trepidation. She wanted to avoid the idea of her ex being on the yacht, but the reality differed from her wishes.

Sasha was on a gorgeous yacht and wanted to enjoy every minute of it. She found herself in front of the mirror in the washroom fixing her hair and makeup and talking to herself.

"Oh. Vian doesn't care and Robin doesn't even remember me. Why am I taking all the stress?" Sasha looked out at the ocean. There were twenty people on the yacht. Sasha was in a yellow dress and had a bathing suit underneath it. She was loving the vibe on the boat. The sun was shining bright and the music was on. Everyone had a glass of champagne in their hands.

Meanwhile, Vian was in his swim shorts and took a dip in the water. He came out of the water and wiped himself with a towel. Sasha found herself irresistibly drawn to him. He was her present and she must embrace this beautiful relationship.

The yacht sailed on the sparkling blue waters. Life was just perfect. Everyone was busy talking. Robin was there with a glass of champagne in his hand.

"Sasha. You want to go change into a swimsuit?" Vian asked Sasha.

"Sure. I will be back." She passed him her glass and walked toward the lower deck.

Robin followed her.

It was just him and her on the lower deck.

"Sasha, stop. Can I talk to you for a second?"

The music was loud on the yacht. Robin was in the cabin with Sasha.

"Congratulations, Tara. You made it this far," Robin looked into her eyes.

Sasha was a little taken aback. She was not expecting Robin to confront her. She held herself back and replied.

"Tara? Who?" Sasha stopped for a second. Her heart was pounding. She was not ready for this. She held her shoulder high. She was in a yellow cotton summer dress.

"You can hide from the world, but not from me. I know you are not some Sasha, but Tara, whom I made love to many times," Robin sipped his champagne.

"Listen. You might be mistaking me for someone else. Also, you are talking to one of your Board of Directors members right now," Sasha reminded him.

"Come on, Tara. I loved you so much. How can you forget us? I knew it was you the moment I saw you for the first time. I just didn't know how you would react. So, I kept it like this," Robin said it all in one breath. He held Sasha by her arm. Sasha took his hand off.

"Listen, I don't know what you are talking about." Sasha was alone on the lower deck with just Robin. Robin had left her without any warning and never contacted her again. How do you take revenge on someone who betrayed you in love? No revenge is the best revenge. While thoughts of her entire past with Robin ran through her mind, she remained calm and collected. She wanted to punch him the whole time she saw him around. But right then, she had the power to do whatever she wanted.

"Tara, listen to me. My mother was sick and I had to go. I wasn't able to tell you anything. I left on the first flight to Australia. Please. I still love you so much. I am sorry, Tara. I am begging you. There is no one like you. You are my whole world." Robin held her hand and begged as he went down on his knees.

Sasha struggled as Robin held her by her arms.

"Robin, stop this nonsense. I am not Tara, but Sasha. I am Vian's girlfriend. You shouldn't be behaving like this." Sasha tried to walk away.

"Why are you doing this to us? You loved me. Please come back, Tara. I will always love you and forever. I am sorry," Robin begged on his knees.

With a cold and determined expression, Sasha looked Robin in the eye and uttered the words that would cut him to the core. "Robin. Listen up. I never loved you. When we return, I suggest you leave your resignation on my desk." Sasha looked into his eyes and kept her calm as she declared, her voice laced with contempt.

"I never loved you." At that moment, Sasha wanted to shatter any hope or affection Robin might have harbored for her. She wanted him to feel the sting of rejection as she had years ago.

"Of course, you gold digger. What else can anyone expect from you." Robin held Sasha tight by her wrist. Sasha tried to get out, but she couldn't.

"Robin. Let me go," Sasha struggled to get her wrist out of his hands.

She felt suffocated in this cabin on the yacht. Just then, Vian arrived, pulled Robin back, and punched him in the face a few times.

"She is my girlfriend. Stay away." Vian took Sasha back to the upper deck.

Robin had a bruised face. He was drunk and passed out in the cabin. Sasha and Vian went back to the upper deck, and the party continued.

The End

"Why are your bags all packed?" Sasha was back in her apartment. She saw that Ira's things were all over the living room and she was packing.

"I guess it's time for me to go." Ira was packing and emptying out her things. Nikki had already gone to rehab.

"Where are you going?" Sasha questioned her. The living room was a mess. There were things everywhere.

"My visa has expired and I will have to go back." Ira didn't make any eye contact with Sasha.

"Oh. What about extending your visa? You can't just leave after two years."

Sasha was all dressed up to go to her work where she would be working as a director on the company's Board.

"My application was denied. It's good anyway. I will just go back and get married and have kids. Live a simple life," Ira looked at Sasha.

There was silence in the room.

Sasha hugged Ira and then opened the door and left.

Sasha went to her office and saw Cathy.

"Good morning, Sasha. Congratulations on your new position," Cathy got up from her desk and greeted Sasha.

"You are welcome, Cathy."

"I can walk you to your new office," Cathy told Sasha.

"Sure. That will be great." Sasha followed her to the elevator.

"Ma'am. Robin sir left an envelope for you this morning. I have left it on your desk." Cathy and Sasha were talking in the elevator.

"Your office is next to Vian's office," Cathy walked Sasha to her new cabin. Sasha couldn't still believe this was happening. Whatever it was, she was loving every bit of it.

"Thank you, Cathy. I will take on from here." She went to her desk and saw an envelope on it. It was from Robin.

Sasha opened the envelope and found that it was a resignation letter. There was a smile on her face. She got up and went to Vian's cabin.

"Good morning, beautiful," Vian got up from his chair and greeted Sasha with a hug and a kiss. She hugged him back.

"Robin's resignation letter." She handed him the paper.

"Oh. Good. That man needed to be fired for how he treated my queen." He kissed her again.

"Vian, how can you love me so much? You are crazy." Sasha pushed him away.

"Well, you're one of a kind and I adore you," Vian said, taking the paper and putting it in one of the drawers in his cabin.

"So, you are moving in with me?" He questioned Sasha.

"Moving in with you in your penthouse?" She asked.

"Yes. You know you said you could be my housekeeper? I need one," Vian had a quirky smile.

"What happened to your housekeeper?" Sasha was serious.

"Silly, I am joking." Vian kissed her again.

"This is what I am in love with. This innocence you have. Oh, I love you so much."

Sasha and Vian kissed, closing their eyes in absolute peace and harmony.